Yesterday's Gone

DIANE BARDEEN

TATE PUBLISHING
AND ENTERPRISES, LLC

Yesterday's Gone
Copyright © 2016 by Diane Bardeen. All rights reserved.

No part of this publication may be reproduced, stored in a retrieval system or transmitted in any way by any means, electronic, mechanical, photocopy, recording or otherwise without the prior permission of the author except as provided by USA copyright law.

This novel is a work of fiction. Names, descriptions, entities, and incidents included in the story are products of the author's imagination. Any resemblance to actual persons, events, and entities is entirely coincidental.

The opinions expressed by the author are not necessarily those of Tate Publishing, LLC.

Published by Tate Publishing & Enterprises, LLC
127 E. Trade Center Terrace | Mustang, Oklahoma 73064 USA
1.888.361.9473 | www.tatepublishing.com

Tate Publishing is committed to excellence in the publishing industry. The company reflects the philosophy established by the founders, based on Psalm 68:11,
"The Lord gave the word and great was the company of those who published it."

Book design copyright © 2016 by Tate Publishing, LLC. All rights reserved.
Cover design by Nino Carlo Suico
Interior design by Jomar Ouano

Published in the United States of America

ISBN: 978-1-68187-912-3
1. Fiction / Family Life
2. Fiction / Coming Of Age
15.11.30

Dedicated to the Inner Core,
the amazing young people who inspire me every day.

Acknowledgments

Where do I start? Well first I would like to thank my Heavenly Papa for trusting me with His words. I cannot do anything without You. My earthly dad, who encouraged me through this entire process; my humble mama who loved the pages of this book; my brubbies Mike and Dave who are always there to cheer me on. My bestie Yvonne who is my partner in crime, and is always there to make me laugh with crispy mullets and eraser heads, Sheri my eternal sister who owns the real "One Way Cafe." Britani Overman who scaled the pages of this book backward and forward like a professional editor, I cannot thank you enough! Thank you to Claire Kennedy for helping me with the final proofing. You are a grammatic genius! Thank you to Tate Publishing for taking a chance on an unknown author and carrying me gingerly through this process. To Gloire and Katie Ndongala, I could not have been more blessed to have crossed paths with you, you are forever my brother and sister, thank you for loving me through my rough edges and always encouraging me! To Angels of Mercy, and Mary Jo, thank you for letting me use your awesome ministry in my book! To Sam, the real Samantha Hampton who I took pieces of and created Samantha Coal, don't ever forget how much you are loved. To Yoneun Jang, having you in my life while I was writing this was an added blessing! Hannah Bear, thank you for allowing me to love teen fiction with you! And last but certainly not least, the Inner Core and Rebecca "Skills Yo." Your dedication to cultivating, sharpening, and using your gifts and talents for the kingdom has inspired me more than you can imagine, love you all so much, past and present!

1

Home Is Not Where the Heart Is

The road was clearly never going to be paved. I could see dirt particles floating in a sandy brown cloud as we traveled closer to Aunt Millie and Uncle Joe's house. It had been a bumpy ride. Jake was silent for almost two hours, and Uncle Joe had a look of constipation on his face as if he didn't know what to say. He was concentrating hard on the road, trying to avoid conversation. It suited me just fine because any kind of talk would have brought reality to my mind, and I had about all I could handle.

I could see the old farmhouse in the distance. The houses in the town of Big Run seemed miles apart. As I looked down at my cell phone, there were no bars available—did not matter, the service was not going to be continued anyway.

"Looks like Millie packed on a few," Jake whispered jokingly. My brother always commented on everyone's appearance.

Millie was standing on the dilapidated porch with one hand positioned on the side of her hip and the other waving us forward. She did look heavier lately, but not overly massive; probably nothing else to do around here but eat! Uncle Joe was a bit of a contrast to Aunt Millie. He was lean and tall with a salt-and-pepper beard. I always thought they resembled a hot dog and hamburger standing next to each other.

Aunt Millie sauntered her way to the car, greeting us as soon as the car stopped. "Oh, Sam, bless your little heart what a beautiful lady you are, and, Jake, ah, Jake, what a fine young man you are!" Aunt Millie was talking as if we hadn't seen each other just a few days ago.

"Why don't you two follow Uncle Joe to your new rooms?" Aunt Millie looked all too excited about this, so I mustered up the best smile I could. "Okay, Aunt Mimi." I called her Mimi ever since I was little because I couldn't pronounce Millie.

As I carefully stepped onto the porch, the door to the old farmhouse opened and a giant dog the size of a small horse almost knocked me over! "Now there, Beetle, simmer down and let the young folk get through the door!" Those were the first words Uncle Joe had spoken since we had been picked up.

As I made my way down the wooden hallway to my "new" bedroom, I could smell the fresh dairy air coming through the windows. It had the smell of fresh linen, grass, and cow manure. *I can't figure out if the smell is offensive or inviting.* My room was freshly painted in a light blue; I liked the color and appreciated the fact that my aunt was trying to make us feel welcome.

"Jake!" I shouted as I nearly fell off the bed while he bulldozed his way next to me. "You almost knocked me over!" I must have been daydreaming because I did not see him coming.

"Sam, you look stoned!" Jake had a way of making light of every situation, no matter how good or bad. "Yeah well, I'm *tired*. How's your room look?" I asked with a less enthusiastic tone.

"It's got a bed and four walls, not much to it, but at least we don't have to share!" Jake said as he made funny faces all too close to my face.

Jake was two years younger than me, and at fourteen, you would still think he is still twelve. He was starting to look more and more like my dad—handsome with strong cheekbones, sandy brown hair, blue eyes, and a chin butt dimple.

Jake left the room, and I was glad to have time by myself to sit and sulk. I looked out the window, and all I could see was Pennsylvania fields of trees and cornstalks. It was October and the beautiful colors of the leaves were falling from the trees in a rhythmic manner. It was pretty, I guess, much different from my view from the high rise we lived in with dad. I already missed the city. It had only been a few hours since we left, but it felt like a lifetime already. Nothing could replace New York, nothing could replace the smell of fresh rolls coming from the bakery in the morning, and nothing could replace my dad. As tears streamed down my face, I could feel a sense of panic coming over me. What the heck happened? It was just last week at this very time, my dad, Jake, and I were laughing over a stupid Adam Sandler film! Why? Why is he gone! I couldn't help but retrace the steps in my head over and over again.

Last Monday, I was walking home from school; my school, the place I had grown to love so much was now gone from my life forever. It may as well have never even existed. When I got home from school that day, my Aunt Mimi and my Uncle Joe greeted me at the door. It had been about two years since I had seen them last. They weren't wearing the usual cheery expressions; they had pain-stricken looks instead. That's when I knew the news was not going to be good. I remembered that type of expression all too well from when my dad told Jake and I my mother had left and was not coming back. Aunt Mimi then shared the news that was forever going to change our lives. My dad had been in a massive car accident on the Jersey Bridge on his way to an appointment. He died at the scene of the accident. I had the same heart pain I felt right now—an overwhelmingly freakish feeling of panic that rushes in to the point of barely being able to breathe.

"Sam," Millie said with a concerned tone outside my door.

"Yes, Aunt Mimi?" I said as I quickly wiped the tears from my face. "Are you settled in? We are almost ready for dinner."

I didn't know how long I had been sitting in the dark, nor do I recall when the daylight had left. "Yes, I'm settling in, I'll be out in a few," I said in the most light-hearted voice I could muster.

After a dinner in almost silence, except the horrific burp Jake let out, I said good night to everyone and went to my room. I blamed my unusually tired demeanor on the trip, and my aunt and uncle accepted it and let me be. The truth is, I didn't want to look at anyone or anything. I just wanted to crawl under the sheets and be welcomed into a dream where my life was back to normal, and my dad greeted me with eggs and bacon in the morning.

"Sam, you're going to be late for school, time to get up!"

So much for dreaming, reality sucks.

Aunt Millie sounded rather frantic, so I pulled myself out of bed and started to get ready.

After a lukewarm shower, I put on my favorite jeans, pulled my auburn hair back into a low ponytail, and glanced in the mirror that was leaning up against my bedroom wall. My dad always said I looked just like my mother when she was my age. I didn't see it. My mother was built like a model with brown hair, legs for days, and dark brown eyes. I have her eyes, her symmetrical face, and thick long hair, but not her legs nor her hourglass shape. I was thin, but I couldn't fill out a pair of jeans or fitted shirt like my mother.

"Here goes nothing," I said to myself and walked out into a warm smelling atmosphere.

Jake was shoveling his face with a stack of pancakes as I plopped myself down into the seventies-style kitchen chair. Aunt Millie rested a plate full of pancakes and eggs in front of me. "Thanks, Aunt Millie, but I'm not really hungry," I said while watching a horrific display of pure gluttony as Jake ate like it was his last meal.

"Nonsense, Sam, you need energy for the day," Aunt Millie said with a concerned look. Her frown turned up as I mustered up enough appetite to eat the eggs.

"Now, kids, I know this is your first day of school here, but we have to drive to the bus stop so you can make it to Punxsutawney High on time, and we don't want to be late." Aunt Millie was packing up our lunches and running around the house in a frenzy. I hated being called a *kid*. I'm sixteen years old and not a kid!

Apparently, the town of Big Run didn't have a high school, just an elementary school, so we had to commute to Punxsutawney High. We were already out in the middle of nowhere, so I was hoping that maybe the school wouldn't feel so *Little House on the Prairie*.

"Aunt Millie, where's Uncle Joe?" Jake asked as he peered out the window trying to find him.

"He's up at 5:00 a.m. every morning tending to the animals and the corn fields. You'll have to get up at the crack of dawn to eat breakfast with your uncle," Millie said with a small grin on her face.

"Oh, heck no, I'm no farmer!" Jake said in a mocking Southern accent. I shot him a look of disapproval and his face turned red.

Aunt Millie put on her shoes and held the door for us, ignoring Jake's rude comment.

The ride to town was only about five minutes long, although it felt longer because of the lack of civilization. I could feel the butterflies starting as the bus pulled up to the stop where the locals were patiently waiting. I had on my favorite jeans, a pretty blue fitted V-neck T-shirt, and my black Nike sneaks with a blue logo. I wasn't dressed to impress by any means, but I was comfortable. I also wasn't prepared to see the array of styles that greeted me in the line to board the bus.

Jake and I jogged up to the bus stop. As we were boarding, I couldn't help but stare at the Goth-styled girl in front of me who had a look of pure disgust on her face as she turned around and peered into my eyes. I looked back at Jake who was flattening out his wrinkled Hollister shirt and faded blue jeans. Aunt Millie was waving frantically from the car with a giant smile across her face. It was nice to have someone who genuinely cared for us, but I couldn't help but imagine it was my dad's warm smile sending me off.

As I boarded the bus, I found an empty seat and made room for Jake to sit down, but he kept going toward the back of the bus! I let out a sigh, closed my eyes, and imagined I was walking to the School of the Arts with my best friend Kate deep in conversation over her drama- filled romance with Mike Shuller. I used to get so bored hearing about their undying love for each other one day and their break up the next, but I would do just about anything to hear her voice right now. I was choking up and feeling a bit sorry for myself as we entered into the town of Punxsutawney.

Through my tear-stained face, I could see the school in the distance. It was bigger than the School of the Arts where I *used* to attend; this school sort of resembled what I would think of as a juvenile delinquent center. The School of the Arts was in a beautiful old building with high ceilings and amazing architecture throughout the halls and classrooms. I missed my school, I missed my friends, and I missed my life.

The bus came to a screeching halt, and I jumped up to see where Jake had landed, just in time to see him fist pumping a boy with dark hair and long bangs. It looked as if Jake had already made a friend. He didn't seem to upset by the move, but he barely spoke or showed any emotion at the funeral last week. How could he be so content already?

The mad rush of students pouring into the building was so intimidating I was short of breath.

"Sam, come on, let's go!" Jake was pulling me by my white and purple Vera Bradley book bag my dad had gotten me last Christmas.

"Knock it off, Jake! If you tear this, I'll tear your face!" I was a little taken back by my response, and so was Jake, by the look of shock on his face.

"Geez, Sam, lighten up! We need to go to the office to get our schedules!"

I followed closely behind Jake as if he knew where he was going.

Aunt Millie had registered us at the school last week immediately after they met with my father's lawyer. My dad left us in the custody of her and my uncle. My father had no family left on his side. Aunt Millie and Uncle Joe were actually the ones who raised my mother. My dad grew up in Big Run just like my mother, and he lost his parents while he was in college, both died within one year of each other to cancer. I never even met my grandparents on my dad's side. I used to imagine they were fantastic and would spoil Jake and me at every holiday. My mother never knew her dad. My grandmother was sixteen when she gave my mom up for adoption, leaving my mom to her older sister, my Aunt Millie. Like mother like daughter, I guess, always on the run, leaving all their responsibility in the hands of others.

The school smelled like a hospital with a light-green, faded tile floor. The walls looked freshly painted and had student artwork framed all the way down the halls. The office was easy to find; we walked up to the counter to a lady that resembled a life-size Marge Simpson. Her hair wasn't blue, but it was a charcoal gray and twisted up in a large bun that sat on the top of her head. I wonder if anyone ever told her how absolutely cartoonish she looked.

"Hi ya'll! What can I do ya for?" the lady said with a high-pitched hillbilly accent.

I didn't know whether to laugh or cry. *Am I in some sort of a theatrical comedy?* I thought. "Um, hi, my name is Samantha Coal, and this is my brother Jake. My Aunt Mimi, I mean Millie Anderson, registered us last week." I was waiting for a response when the lady's smiling face turned into a frown.

"Oh, I'm so sorry, you poor dears, I'm so sorry about your father!"

The lady was looking back and forth from Jake and me waiting for a reaction. I was getting those heart palpitations again and was furious with my aunt for telling this stranger!

"Yeah, thanks, can we please get our schedules, Ms. Fats, is it?" Jake said in a sarcastic manner while squinting his eyes, pretending he was having a hard time reading the nameplate that sat on the front desk.

"It's pronounced Fates, please," the secretary said with her lips pursed together.

"Oh, so sorry, Ms. Fats, I mean, Fates," Jake said with a wry smirk on his face.

I wanted to laugh out loud! Obviously Jake was annoyed by her announcement to everyone in the office about our personal and private information. *The last thing I want is sympathy from strangers!*

"Here you go. Jake, you need to report to room 306 on the third floor, and, Sam, you need to report to room 113. These are your first period classes. You have five minutes between classes, and if you need any further assistance, please feel free to stop back in the office, and we will be happy to assist you." Ms. Fatz became very businesslike after the way Jake made a mockery of her name.

My first-period class was Biology. Great, I hated science. Jake had gym; he was happy enough to be able to romp around, getting all his crazy energy out. He played baseball for junior varsity last year when he was in eighth grade. I, on the other hand, had dance classes for my physical education at SOTA. I was not looking forward to a regular gym class. Jake ran up the stairs and was gone from my life for the day. Feeling a bit awkward, nervous, and downright angry that I had to walk into first period late as the *new girl*, I opened the door to room 113.

"Well, what do we have here?" said a tall thin man with a pointy nose and short brown hair. "Hi, I'm Sam, I'm new this is my first day." I said in a tiny voice, to the point I was now embarrassed. *I sound like a moron.*

I hadn't even looked at the class yet, but I could feel their eyes peering at me, scoping my every movement. "Well, well, well, I'm Mr. Sullivan, and welcome to Bio 101. You can have a seat over there next to Mariah in the second row. You can share a text with her today, I will have a book for you on Wednesday."

The way the school operated was somewhat college style. They didn't have the same classes every day but extended classes every other day. I politely nodded and quickly walked over to the only empty seat in the class. My heart was beating out of my chest, and I could feel my face flush.

"Hi," I said to the pretty brunette next to me. She was thin with a round face and curly hair.

"Hey," she said with a welcoming smile. That calmed me down a bit, enough to pull out a notebook and try to focus on what the teacher was talking about.

The room was set up with lab tables and two students sat at each table. I was seated next to a window and was captivated by the well-manicured football and baseball fields. It was clear that sports were important to the school; I was sure Jake would fit in just fine.

Before I knew it, the bell rang, and I quickly pulled out my schedule, I couldn't stop my hands from shaking. My next period was a study hall on the second level in room 225.

The halls were filled with friends chatting a mile a minute. It was so crammed I was hugging my bag as if I would not survive without it. I was looking down at my feet while climbing the stairs; the next thing I knew, I was head butting the person in front of me. Apparently, the flow of traffic stopped without my knowledge, embarrassing to say the least.

"I usually shake hands when I'm meeting someone for the first time. Now I know what Charlie feels like." The tall boy in front of me whose bottom I just ran into was now smiling back at me.

"Um, hey, sorry, I wasn't paying attention," I said as my face was burning red with embarrassment. "No problem, haven't seen you before. Are you new to this stairwell?"

I cannot believe he is going to try to carry on a conversation in the middle of the stairs. Did he not feel the elbows digging into his side as he stood there? I for sure as heck do! And who the heck is Charlie? "Um, yeah, I just started today," I said as I started to move forward, passing him. "Sorry, I don't want to walk in late to my next class," I said, passing him by. I looked over my shoulder, and he was still smiling at me…creep.

Room 225 was just around the corner from the stairs. I was glad to see kids just walking in. I found a seat safely toward the back of the room. Just as I started to settle in, I saw those familiar blue eyes peering at me, moving closer until his head butted bottom stole the seat right next to me.

"I'd like to introduce my better side. I'm Sam," the tall boy said as he continued to smile. *Great, we have the same name!* "Hi, I'm Samantha." I tried to look like I was busy, not used to meeting people in such an awkward state.

Sam was tall, thin, with brown, tousled hair, and of course, those blue eyes. He was handsome in a way, not drop dead, but definitely easy to look at. I didn't care; I didn't want to be friendly with anyone right now…just wanted to get through this godforsaken first day!

"By the way, Charlie is my dog," Sam said, getting his books out.

"Oh, ha… I get it now," I said, trying to sound amused. *Nice, he was referencing me to sniffing his butt like a dog, and I thought I felt awkward before.*

As the teacher did roll call, I realized I didn't have anything to do. I had no biology book yet, and I hadn't been to any other classes yet. I took out my notebook to doodle when I felt my pants buzzing. My phone was working! Without thinking, I pulled it out and looked at the dozens of missed calls and texts! They were from my friends—mostly Kate. I was fighting back tears reading numerous texts of how she missed me and how life was not the same, how she and Mike broke up again in the first couple of texts but were back together toward the end. For a quick minute, my world felt normal again.

"Eh, em, excuse me, miss. We do *not* allow cell phones in this classroom. Please bring it to me."

I never even bothered to introduce myself to the study hall monitor when I walked in; I was too busy trying to blend in. She was portly with a pretty face and too much lipstick. "I'm sorry, I didn't know," I mustered out while walking to the front of the class. I placed it in her hands and proceeded to walk back to my seat, not making eye contact with anyone. The bell did not come soon enough. I marched back up to the teacher, and she handed me my phone while keeping eye contact with me to let me know she was watching me—ridiculous.

My stomach was making gurgling sounds; thank God it was time for lunch. I guess. The dreaded lunchroom, finding a seat and not feeling like such a dork with no friends. I wished Jake had lunch the same time I did.

The lunchroom was on the first floor close to my locker, so it was easy to find. I walked in to the sea of students filling the large windowed cafeteria with laughter, shouting, and in the corner of the room, there was a small gathering of girls that were cheering! *Oh, brother, puhlease get me out of here!*

"Sam, is it? Come and sit with us, there's plenty of room." *The girl from first period, the pretty brunette was welcoming* me *to her table. Ahhhh, such a relief!*

"Thanks, I think I'll take you up on it!" I said as I sat next to a pretty blond girl with a big smile. "Hi, I'm Rachel, and this is Pat, Jade, and you seem to already know Mariah, and of course, we can't forget Sam. *As if I hadn't seen Sam enough, I was now about to share the same lunch table.*

"Ahhh, we meet again," Sam said with that same smirk as earlier during my huge embarrassing failure on the staircase.

"Yeah, lucky you I'm not walking behind you with your lunch tray in hand!" I laughed generously. I figured I might as well be friendly; I had been lucky enough to have been welcomed so kindly on my first day!

"Um, I'm not even going to ask." Rachel said referencing the other Sam's comment while opening her white paper lunch bag and pulled out an apple, carrot sticks, and a granola bar. I was terrified to open my lunch bag; I never even looked at what Aunt Millie packed me! All I could think about was that giant breakfast full of carbs, fat, and sugar!

"I'm Samantha, It's my first day here, I just moved to Big Run yesterday." I was hoping that no one would ask for detailed info. I peered into my oversized lunch bag.

"What brings you here to Punxsutawney High?" Pat who was seated directly across from me asked with his face scrunched up as if he couldn't understand why I would move out into the middle of nowhere, like I had a choice in the matter.

"My brother and I moved here with my Aunt Millie and Uncle Joe," I replied as I was now focused on the large mystery sandwich inside of my bag, a Rubbermaid container full of applesauce, an orange, two chocolate chip cookies, and a bag of Doritos, enough for two people to eat.

I looked up and all eyes were on me, I could feel my cheeks turn red, and I was getting those heart palpitations again. I have never been so nervous so many times in my entire life! Why were they staring at me? My ginormous lunch? Were they waiting for more information? What? Then the fated question arose, the one I did not want to answer.

"Is it Millie and Joe Anderson?" Mariah asked.

"Yes! How do you know them?" I said with a puzzled look on my face.

"Oh, they are friends of the family. We go way back. Why did you move here with your aunt and uncle?" Mariah politely asked, her blue eyes sparkling with sincerity.

Do I really have to go there on the first day here? I do not want friends out of pity!

"Um, well...my..."Before I could answer, the girl they called Jade saved the day, redirecting focus onto her.

"What is he doing with her? Are you kidding me! He said he needed space! I'll give him space right between his eyes!" Jade was now standing halfway up with her fists resting on the lunch table.

Mariah was looking back and forth from the boy Jade was talking about and Jade, not knowing what to do. Everyone at the table were giving each other knowing eyes; something told me Jade was the last to know about the boy and the tall, thin, blond he was walking with hand in hand.

Jade collapsed back into her seat, and Mariah moved next to her for comfort.

"I don't get it? Why would Peter do this to me? Jade's face turned five different shades of red before the tears started coming.

I felt uncomfortable to say the least. I didn't even know these people. I just sat there, looking apologetic, not saying a word while everyone else was trying to make her feel better. Not long after the bell rang and I was on to the rest of my day.

Finally my last class was Geometry, and I was lucky enough to get a book. I must have daydreamed my way through the class because when the bell rang, I was so startled I nearly jumped out of my seat! Finally I get to go home—well, what home is now.

The ride home was so much easier—no butterflies, no knots, at least I could go hibernate in my own room! Jake actually sat next to me on the bus on the way home, talking incessantly about the school grounds and the baseball field. He was very excited about trying out for baseball when it came time. I guess in the city he was deprived of green. Aunt Millie had freshly baked chocolate chip cookies for us when we got home—that was something I only saw on movies or watching re-runs of the *Brady Bunch*; it was a nice change.

After dinner, I sat in the old rocking chair on the half-fixed porch, starring out into the sky full of stars. I could get used to seeing the beauty of the night unclouded by pollution. Even though we were only a few hours away from the city, it felt like worlds apart. New York was full of excitement but definitely had its limits with soaking in natural beauty. My heart still ached for the not so long ago past; after dinner with Dad, we would watch TV together, eating popcorn or ice cream. Kate would be texting me nonstop, planning for the next school day, or a weekend adventure. Life most definitely would never be the same.

2

The New Normal

The next day, the butterflies seemed to be less invasive on my digestive pattern. I was on time for every class. *BBRRRINGGG.* The school bell announced that it was lunchtime, and I was anticipating having to face the lunch crew for the second time, braving the fateful question of why I moved here. I had worked on my speech all morning as to how I would answer.

"Hi, everyone, mind if I sit with y'all again?" *Why in the world did I just say ya'll!* I glanced quickly at everyone for approval but noticed that Jade was not anywhere to be seen.

"Sure, Samantha, right? You don't have to ask, just make yourself at home!" Mariah said with a giant smile. She was so beautiful and sweet! Back in the city, the ones with the least amount of imperfections usually had their nose so high up in the air; they couldn't smell their own stench. *It is nice being around beautiful girls that are so welcoming!*

"Thanks!" I plopped myself down next to Rachel, and she politely made room for me. I peered into my lunch bag, hoping for a bit more of normalcy, when I felt eyes were glued to my every movement. Sam was staring at me.

"Are you afraid that something is going to jump out at you?" Sam asked with a snarky look on his face.

"No. I am just not used to packed lunches, and my aunt Millie likes to make sure that I have enough to feed a table full of people," I said, looking for approval from anyone.

"Oh, tell me about it, my grandma makes sure that no one leaves the house without feeling like a stuffed turkey!" Pat replied with food in his mouth, as he took three huge bites of his sandwich. *Boys can be so gross.*

"Are you guys all going to Amped tonight?" Mariah asked the group as they nodded their heads to say yes to her question. "Sam, are you busy tonight?" Mariah asked, and everyone's eyes were now all on me.

"What's Amped?" I said with a curious look on my face. *Great, my first invite out! I can't believe I am being so welcomed in!* Then she said the dreaded words.

"It's my youth group, we meet every Wednesday night. You should come, it's fun and our youth pastor is amazing." Mariah was waiting for my reply, and so was everyone else. I could feel my face getting beet red; I wasn't sure how to answer this except that God and I...we were not on good terms. I did not have much to do with Him after my mom left, and now that my dad was gone, I could not imagine a God that would take both parents from two children that needed them desperately—no way was I going to some Jesus-loving youth group!

"Um…I don't think I could make it, we just got settled here, me and my brother Jake, and uh, we really need to help my aunt settle everything at home." *There, I did it. Now the question was would they accept my rejection?*

"That's okay, maybe next time," Sam said with a quick wink. *Whew! Dodged a bullet there.*

"Okay, well, I guess we will see you at church on Sunday then!" Mariah said with an even bigger smile.

"I am not so sure about that, ya know my aunt and uncle are really into family and they like to spend time with us." The lies started pouring out, the truth is my brother and I had only been here for a couple of nights. I had no idea how they spend their time!

"Oh, we will definitely see you on Sunday. Your Aunt Millie and Uncle Joe never miss a Sunday service, well, except for last week that is," Mariah said with a questioning gaze.

"Oh, okay, I wasn't aware that they attended your church," I said, trying not to sound too disappointed. *How was I going to get around this one? Would Aunt Millie and Uncle Joe force me to go? They had better not!*

Mariah, Pat, Sam, and Rachel were all in deep conversation about their youth group and upcoming events; I felt kind of bad that I was so quick to reject their offer. They had been so kind, more welcoming than anyone else in the school had been. I just could not go there, and I wanted nothing to do with church and all that crap; honestly I had no idea how anyone could buy into a God that allows such horrible things to happen to good people. All I knew is I wanted nothing to do with a God like that; I was better off on my own.

....

Saturday morning could not have come quicker, being our first full weekend here, I did not know what to expect. As I carefully tiptoed down the hall into the kitchen, I was greeted by Beetle barking as if he'd seen a ghost. "Quiet, Beetle, I don't want to wake anyone!" My senses told me that I was not the first one awake; the smell of fresh brewed coffee was filtering through my nostrils. I made it to the kitchen to see Aunt Mimi sitting at the table sipping a hot cup of coffee, reading a book, with a huge smile on her face.

"Good morning, Sam, are you hungry?" Aunt Mimi was up on her feet faster than you could say boo.

"Not really. I have a hard time eating first thing in the morning, I guess my body needs to catch up to my mind." I really had no explanation, but even as a younger child, I needed to be up for a while before I could eat.

"Okay, darling, just let me know when and I'll scratch ya up a batch of those eggs you like so much." Aunt Mimi's eyes danced when she smiled. I had no idea why she could be so cheerful all the time. She lived in an old house with a husband that barely spoke, she had an estranged sister who left her to care for her troubled child, who then abandoned her own children, and now, she was the prize owner of two teenagers who are most likely damaged goods. *What did she have so much to smile about?*

"Where's Uncle Joe?" I asked as I looked out the window to catch a possible viewing.

"He and your brother went to town to get supplies," Aunt Mimi said.

"Oh, Jake is up?" *I cannot believe I slept in later than Jake!*

Aunt Mimi just smiled as she watched me process. "Yep, he was up early, had breakfast with your uncle and out the door he went!"

"Oh, wow. He is usually not a morning person, especially on the weekend!"

Uncle Joe was a man of few words. He never spoke much, but man did he work! At times you could catch Aunt Mimi watching out the window, shaking her head, always saying that Uncle Joe needed to hire on someone to help around with the farm. Maybe Jake will fill that gap. It made me feel kind of guilty, knowing we were now costing them more money.

I don't know how long I had been standing there in a daydream, but Aunt Mimi was looking at me with questioning eyes.

"Honey, come and sit down here and chat with me for a bit," Aunt Mimi said with a tender tone.

I obediently took the chair across from her, nervous about what she might ask. I was not in the mood to cry or tell anyone the turmoil that had been making my stomach knotted over the past couple weeks. I was not in the mood to talk about Dad, my first week here at school, or the fact that my best friends are no longer reachable. I was just not in the mood. But I was definitely not prepared for what she was about to ask.

"Sam, have you ever been to church?" Aunt Mimi was resting her hand on mine.

"Um, well yeah, I mean when we were real little, I can remember going as a family, when Mom was still with us," I said as I could feel the heat rising to my face, embarrassed that I can still feel anything for a woman who would leave her family.

"Oh, that's right, I almost forgot about that. It was a little church outside of the city, right?" Aunt Mimi was squinting, concentrating on her memory.

"Yeah, I think so. I really can't remember. I was so little. I can remember the singing and the way I felt when Mom would drop me off at the nursery. I gave her quite a hard time. I never wanted to be away from her." *What is going on! Why am I feeling like this? All I want to do was ball my eyes out.*

"I'm so sorry, honey, the last thing I want to do is cause you any more pain. I am just asking because we would like you and your brother to join us for church tomorrow morning. There is no pressure, but I wanted to let you know that they have a very large youth group, and they even have a dance troop!" Aunt Mimi said.

As if that would entice me. "Oh, you haven't done anything wrong, I just am not sure, can I think about it?" *Heck no! I do not want to go anywhere near a church is what I wanted to shout!*

"Of course you can. You can take as much time as you need. I just want you to know that God loves you so much, and so do I," Aunt Mimi said, throwing one of her "feeling sorry for me" type of smiles.

Well, I didn't need pity; I needed to be back home with Dad, my best friend, the school that I loved, and a city that never slept! But that was not going to happen, so I settled for a lukewarm shower and some scrambled eggs, and Beetle decided to be my new best friend. *The giant mutt follows me everywhere I go!*

A couple hours later, Jake and Uncle Joe came home with a bunch of supplies and some grocery's Aunt Millie had asked for. I was happy to see Jake; as much as he can be annoying, he is the closest thing I have left to normalcy.

"What's up, sis!" Jake shouted and put his face close up into mine.

"You're annoying really. And geez did you forget to brush your teeth this morning." I said with a big smile. *Jake is usually always happy and full of energy.*

"Brush my teeth you ask? 'Round these parts, we don't need to brush our teeth! That's what some of dere black diner coffee is fur, right, Uncka Joe?" Jake said, pulling his jeans up above his waist, pushing out his stomach, and resting his thumbs through the loopholes of his jeans, and turning back to Uncle Joe. Uncle Joe just nodded his head, waved his hand over his head, but I did notice a smirk in the corner of his mouth.

"You're such a dork!" I said and could not hold in the laughter.

Aunt Millie, myself, and Jake had a bit of a laugh together after that; Jake was always good for putting a smile on everyone's face. It was the first real laughter I was able to let out in the past couple of weeks.

Boy, was I glad later that evening for the groceries Aunt Millie asked for! After a delicious dinner of roasted chicken, garlic sautéed Brussels sprouts, mashed potatoes, and freshly baked apple pie for dessert; we landed in the living room to watch a movie. It wasn't New York, it wasn't my dad, but it did make me feel comfortable to say the least.

After the movie ended, Uncle Joe and Aunt Mimi quickly got up and started to tidy up the living room, mumbling about, getting up early to get the bagels and coffee.

"Aunt Mimi, why are you getting up early on Sunday for bagels? Your pancakes are better than any kind of breakfast I can imagine!" Jake said with a look of worry that he wasn't going to be able to pound a full stack of pancakes in the morning.

"Oh, Jake, tomorrow is Sunday, your uncle Joe and I pick up the bagels at the bakery and make the coffee before Sunday school starts every week," Aunt Mimi said with a look of remorse that she hadn't said anything sooner.

"Oh, I see, what time do you leave in the morning?" Jake asked with a questioning gaze.

"We leave here around 8:15 a.m. to get the bagels and get the coffee started before people start to trickle in at church for Sunday school," Aunt Mimi said while squinting at Uncle Joe, making sure he was folding up the afghan the right way.

"We would love you and your sister to join us! I already spoke to Sam about it, I wanted to talk to you too Jake but it slipped my mind—probably a little too much apple pie!" Aunt Mimi said with a little giggle.

Jake looked at me with a puzzled look. I must have had a look of horror on my face; I gave him a willful look. I was hoping he would catch on; we could use a morning to ourselves to talk. I wanted to hear about his week without anyone there. I wanted to feel free to express how I was feeling!

"Sure, I'll try anything once…what kind of bagels do ya get? Any cream cheese?" Jake said with a playful smile. Well, I guess he did not get my hint! Darn his stomach! Aunt Mimi looked so pleased I thought she was going to burst; Uncle Joe nodded his head as if Jake said the smartest thing on the earth.

"Sam, you gonna go?" Jake asked without really making eye contact with me.

At this point, I was furious with him! They would have to drag me there by my hair!

"Na, I think I'll pass. I'm tired, and I really don't want to get up early after my first week here. Good night, everyone," I said with a jerk of my head as I swiftly arose from the floral patterned sofa.

I left the room with everyone staring at me. I didn't care, I was about to lose it, and I didn't want them to see the tears starting in the corners of my eyes.

....

I woke to the sound of birds chirping, with the sun getting ready to pop. I could smell the bar of Caress lather coming from the bathroom next to me. Aunt Mimi was probably in the shower. I was fighting the urge to go to the bathroom, knowing my excuse for staying home to sleep in would no longer be sufficient. I held on as long as I could but ended up running to the bathroom just in time to see Aunt Mimi come out in a large towel.

"Sam, you're up!" Aunt Mimi said with a smile as if it wasn't awkward seeing her in a towel.

"Yeah, when you gotta go ya gotta go," I said as I darted past her into the steam-fresh bathroom just in time. Now what was I going to say! As I sat there contemplating, I made a rash decision and hopped into the shower and proceeded to get ready for church. Like Jake said, "I'll try anything once."

3

Weird

The whitewashed building was old, and you could smell the aging wood crackle as you walked across the floor. It was very Little House on the Prairie.

"Stop twitching, Sam!" Jake pushed my hands and shook his head as he led us down the aisle in between the old wooden pews. Sometimes, I must admit, *I* was much younger than Jake when it came to being adventurous. How was he able to take new things with such ease?!

Aunt Mimi and Uncle Joe were getting the coffee brewing for Sunday school. So Jake and I ventured into the sanctuary to wait for the "festivities" to start. I didn't want to even be here. How did I get myself into this? Stupid bladder! Too much change is bad for the soul, right? As we made our way down the aisle, there was a middle-aged woman in a polite-looking pantsuit flipping through her Bible on the podium in the front. Jake and I made ourselves comfortable midway up in the pews and sat quietly. After a few minutes, the woman glanced over at us with squinting eyes.

"Oh, I didn't see you two there! You must be Millie and Joe's niece and nephew!" the smile-stricken lady said as she swiftly walked toward Jake and me.

"Yes, that's us," Jake replied as he stood up to shake her hand. I followed suit and returned a nice firm grip to the friendly woman. *Why does everyone know who the heck we are!*

"My name is Pauline, welcome to Church of Love Assembly of God. We are so glad you could make it today!" The woman named Pauline said with a plastered smile—that oddly enough seemed genuine.

"Hi, I'm Sam."

"And I'm Jake," we said and sat back down.

"Well, if you want to stay for my Sunday school class, you are more than welcome, but they do have a youth Sunday school class downstairs in the youth room. Pastor Gloire is here now if you would like to meet him!"

I could hardly contain my excitement—a pastor named Gloire, great! If he was a cheese ball, I was going to make a run for it.

"Sure," Jake said with just about as much apprehension as I was feeling.

Not more than a second later, a dark-skinned man wearing a Teenage Mutant Ninja Turtle T-shirt came walking down the middle aisle toward us.

"Ah, there you are! Just in time," the kind woman said as she started waving him toward us.

"Pastor Gloire, this is Jake and Sam, they are here with Millie and Joe," she said while giving him a knowing look.

Do people really think we are that juvenile that we are not going to pick up on social cues? Obviously they know why we are here. I just want to crawl into a whole and wake up from this nightmare!

"Hey, guys, welcome! You can call me Gloire, you don't have to call me pastor if you don't want, not much into titles!" The smile-plastered younger-looking man said as he greeted us not with just a handshake, but a huge hug—*Not used to that on a first greeting!*

"Hey," Jake said and put his hands in the pockets of his blue jeans, obviously a little uncomfortable. *Finally, I'm not the only one!*

"Can you two help me with something?" Gloire asked while waving us in his direction, not waiting for a reply.

Jake and I followed Gloire out of the sanctuary into a small room off to the side. He motioned us to pick up large brown boxes that were stacked in the corner. We then followed him downstairs into a large dark room. Before I could open my mouth to ask where he wanted the boxes, the lights came on and the room lit up. I was not prepared for what I saw; it was not your typical "church" setting. The room was two-toned, the bottom part of three of the walls were painted white with tons of posters plastered on them. The top part was painted black! The black part of the walls had tons of words written all over them in neon and pastel colors. The ceiling had giant planets, CDs, and fluorescent stars hanging from it. In the far end of the room was a beautifully stained bar that reached the length of the wall, with bar stools lining perfectly across, with mini white lights across the lip under the bar. There were tables that looked like giant spools near the bar area with tailor made wooden chairs around each table. On the right side of the room, the top part of the wall was lined with mirrors and a dance bar, and there was a hard wooden floor in the carpet that reached the length of the dance bar. The left and middle part of the room had chairs lined up theater style that faced a stage. Around the perimeter of the room, there were oversized chairs that looked like as much fun to jump into as a giant pile of leaves. The room. Was. Awesome.

It took me a minute to soak everything in, but the realization of holding this giant box helped me out of the trance, as it fell to the floor.

"I'm so sorry! I hope there is nothing breakable in this!" as I reached down to pick up the box, Gloire met me at the base of the box and picked it up.

"No worries! I am sorry I didn't take it from you. I was enjoying the expression on both of your faces as you looked at the room, we are thrilled with the renovations down here, and I get a little overexcited showing new people."

"Dude, it's fresh," Jake said with an approving nod of his head. It was pretty amazing. If "church" was anything like the feel of this room, maybe it wouldn't be as bad as I thought!

Gloire started telling us how God had sent him here, him and his wife, to help out the church with the youth; it was a little too much to take in. How did God send him? Was he teleported? I mean, come on, do people actually believe this *crap*?

Before I had a chance to ask any questions, kids started piling in down the stairs. I found a seat near the back row of the chairs, hoping to blend in.

"Sam! You're here!" The next thing I knew, there were arms around my neck, and I was being smothered by strangers! When I was able to see daylight again, I saw those beautiful eyes and brunette curls dancing around the perimeter of Mariah's face and other familiar faces from the lunch table, minus the boy Sam. Mariah really was magazine-worthy.

"Yeah, um, my brother and I thought we would give it a try," I said and noticed Jake looking at me with an inquisitive expression on his face from a distance.

"Your brother? Sam, you must introduce!" Mariah said while she pulled me from my comfortable back row seat with as much force as a bulldozer. Jake was talking to Gloire and some of the other kids when Mariah and I bounded into the conversation. Jake was staring at Mariah—*Oh, brother.*

"You must be Sam's brother, I'm Mariah," she said as she slipped out her hand for a handshake. Jake said hello as his face flushed a pinkish red.

Gloire called everyone to be seated and then called up the "worship team." *Can't. Contain. My excitement.* Mariah and her friends pulled me up to the front row, I was not happy, but I appreciated the fact that they seemed genuinely interested in including me in their group. The youth on the stage started with a prayer and then started playing their instruments. The songs at first flowed out up beat, and many of the youth were clapping or bouncing to the beat. The group wasn't half bad; I didn't really understand all the excitement, but I noticed my body starting to sway back and forth, enjoying the beat. The team then started playing slower music, and many of the teens started raising their hands. *What the heck is this about? It was weird.* I noticed Jake in the row behind me in my peripheral, looking about as uncomfortable as I felt.

The words to one of the songs struck me: "I want to be near, near to you heart, loving the world and hating the dark, I want to see dry bones living again, singing as one, hallelujah, holy, holy, who is worthy, God almighty, the great I am."

The song was really beautiful, but what the heck did the lyrics mean? What is "I am"? What does hating the dark mean? Are "Christian" people afraid of the dark? I just don't get it, but the song is really captivating, it makes me feel kinda weird...weird, weird, weird!

"God isn't impressed with going through the motions, young people. He wants to know *you*, all of *you*, not just a piece of your heart, your *whole* heart!" Pastor Gloire was pacing back and forth while he was speaking. Then he stopped dead in his tracks, and I felt his eyes burning through mine.

"He loves you, He cares for you, He wants to meet every need, and all you have to do is submit yourself to Him! Fall in love with Jesus! He died on the cross for you, so you could have eternity with the Father."

After that, I didn't hear the rest of the message... What was he talking about? *Fall in love with Jesus.* I don't get it? Sorry, I would like a boyfriend at some point, but I don't think I want to date the "son of God" or however they say it—kinda creepy and *weird*. Why would *God* love me? And how does he *know* this? My heart was pounding out of my chest; it was the *weirdest* feeling I have ever had. How could I give someone I don't see or know my heart? This was a little much to take in. All I know is, I wanted to make a run for it and never come back, and at the same time, I didn't want to leave. The pounding in my heart wasn't painful; it was unexplainable.

When the message was over, they opened the "bar" and had hot and cold beverages including frappes, lattes, coffee, soft drinks, hot chocolate, and many other drinks you would see at a cafe. They had snacks available as well. They sold them for a very low price, but we (Jake and I), being newbies, had our choice of whatever for free. The money that they made from the sale of drinks went toward some fine arts program they offered for the youth of the community. I ordered some special caramel latte, and Jake ordered a frappe. The youth behind the bar made the drinks like they were baristas at Starbucks; it was pretty cool, I must admit.

The ride home was filled with Aunt Millie's excitement over some outreach the church holds every year to raise money for women and children who have been involved in human trafficking. I had no idea what human trafficking even was until she started to explain it. I just can't believe that there are people out there that would sell another human being for sex…and children? What kind of world do we live in, and what kind of *God* would allow this to happen? My brain started hurting from everything that I had to process.

After a nice early supper, I curled up on the large rocking bench on the porch and let the new October breeze blow the long bangs over my face. It was very peaceful at Aunt Millie and Uncle Joe's—so quiet, in fact, you could hear all the sounds of nature. I was not used to that. In the city, I could hear the sound of traffic, the hustle and bustle of people walking the streets at any time of day, the honking of horns, and music coming from the corner store.

The thought of the city brought me back to a world that in a very short time was now foreign to me. I wondered how Kate was doing, I wondered who was now living in our cozy apartment on Plymouth and Ninth, and who was making sure our neighbor, Mr. Jenson, got his paper in the morning. "Lazy, no-good rascals! Stealing my paper! What do they need it for!" he would shout from his doorway. The truth is, no one ever stole his paper; my dad seemed to think he forgot where he put it every day. So Dad made sure one of us knocked on his door and handed him the paper off the ground; somehow the human interaction made him remember. Dad…I was never going to be able to say that word again and be able to attach it to the living… the thought of that alone made my tear ducts prepare for a waterfall.

"Beetle! Stop licking my face!" The sandy brown mutt must have liked the taste of the salt from my tears. As I stretched out, I noticed the chill in the air and how the sun was creeping its way down for the night. I had no idea what time it was, or how long I had fallen asleep for. The door creaked open, and the closest representation of my father walked out and landed right next to me on the bench.

"Hey, sis, you okay? You've been out for almost three hours," Jake said with a concerned look I wasn't used to.

"Yeah, I'm fine," I said as I managed to get myself in a sitting position. "I was just really tired. My brain has been on overdrive today," I said as I peered into his baby blue eyes. They were softer than normal, and he looked very serious. "What's up?" I asked with a soft nudge from my shoulder to his.

Jake sighed and stared straight ahead.

"I don't know, Sam. It really hit me today that this is our new life. I know that I may act goofy a lot, but it doesn't mean I am not thinking about Dad every day."

I could see tears welling up in his eyes for the first time since we heard the dreaded news. I was searching for the right comforting words to say, but I could think of nothing. We sat together in peaceful silence for quite a while.

"Well, we better get in and settled, back to the beginning of a new week," Jake said non-enthusiastically.

"Yeah, how was your week? I have wanted to talk to you about it all weekend, but we haven't had much time alone," I said while moving my position to face him straight on.

"It wasn't bad, the school has a really nice ball field, and I think I'll try out for the team next year. I met some of the ball players and they seem pretty cool, how about you? How was your week?"

"It was decent. As you know, I met Mariah and some of the kids you met at church today, and they have been very kind to me, including me in their group at lunch and stuff."

We said good night to the soft breeze, and Aunt Millie and Uncle Joe, then headed our separate ways to our rooms. The three-hour nap did not affect my ability to sleep; I was out when I hit the pillow.

4

Tears

Sam, the snarky boy who always seemed to be ever present in my daily grind, was absent today, and he wasn't at church. Mariah mentioned during service yesterday that she was wondering where he was. Not that I *cared*; it was just noticeable. He wasn't there to bother me in class and study hall.

    The lunch bell rang, and I was anticipating my new "usual" crew to bombard me with questions on what I thought of church. I wasn't sure how I was going to respond. When I got to the table they were normally at, no one was there. I sat down and glanced around the cafeteria hoping to see someone familiar, but I found nothing. I could feel the blood rushing to my face; I hated feeling like a loser eating lunch by myself. Where were they? Did I somehow offend them? I opened my lunch, and to my pleasant surprise, I had peach yogurt, an apple, crackers and cheese, and bottled water. Perfect! Aunt Millie really catches on quick. I should wake up early enough to pack my own lunch. I just didn't feel comfortable going through someone else's fridge.

A few minutes later, Mariah and the crew entered the cafeteria and slowly walked over to the table. They looked very sad, and it looked like Mariah had been crying.

"Is everything okay?" I managed to say with a mouth full of yogurt.

Rachel, the pretty blond girl spoke first, "Um yeah, were okay, one of our friends is going through a very rough time."

Mariah blew her nose and then looked at me with her head tilted. "You remember Sam, right?" she asked.

"Yeah, of course, is he okay?" My heart started to panic a bit; he was annoying, but I wouldn't wish anything bad on the kid. He actually was very nice to me.

"He's okay. It's not him, it's his mother," Mariah said while tears were forming in the corner of her eyes."

Pat breathed in heavy. From the camaraderie between Sam and Pat, you could tell they were best friends. He had bloodshot eyes as well, either from lack of sleep or he himself had been crying pretty hard.

"Sam's mom had a brain aneurysm this past Sunday, and she passed away instantly," Pat said and sat gingerly down at the table, tears welling up into his eyes.

I didn't know what to say; I started having trouble breathing. Having gone through something similar just weeks earlier set me apart from my newfound friends; I could relate—I could most definitely relate.

"I'm so sorry, how is Sam doing?" I said very softly.

"I'm not sure. Gloire came to the school this morning to let us know. He said Sam isn't responding to anyone. His father said to give him some time," Mariah said and let her shoulders fall into a slouching position.

Everyone quietly opened their lunch bags; some had nothing, and we nibbled in silence. I wanted to scream! All I could think about was my pain, my dad… I was holding back a force full of tears when the bell finally rang. I was ever so glad for lunch to be over. Everyone said their good-byes, then Mariah turned to me and lightly touched my arm.

"Sam, we are going to meet on Wednesday at Amped and pray for Sam and his family. We want to do something for him, and we are going to brainstorm together. Do you want to come with us?"

"Uh, um, okay, sure, I'll be there," I said with no idea what I was getting myself into.

I quickly scooted out of the lunchroom and bolted toward the closest bathroom; tears were flowing down my face before I reached the door when I heard a familiar voice.

"Sam, what the heck are you running for? Geez, you're gonna knock someone over!" Jake said in a correcting manner. I turned in time to see his stern expression turn into concern. "Hey, are you okay? What happened?"

I lost it. Right there in the middle of the hall, in front of the girls' bathroom. I didn't care. My body slid down the wall until my behind hit the floor. I tucked my knees in and buried my face. I sobbed. Jake sat next to me in silence until a hallway monitor grabbed his attention. Jake and the monitor spoke and then we were alone. No one in the halls, no students gawking and staring at us. We were new to the school; for all they knew, it could have been a couple fighting. I looked up just in time to see Mrs. Fatz.

"Oh dear, what happened to you two? Are you okay?" Mrs. Fatz said in a concerned tone.

"Yeah, thanks, Mrs. Fatz," Jake said, pronouncing her name correctly.

"Well, you two are late for class. Do you need me to write you up passes, or would you like to talk to one of the counselors in the office?" she said with compassion.

I could not imagine what my face looked like, but going to class right then and there was not going to happen, so I took her up on the offer. Jake made sure I was okay and went to class late. I walked in stride with Mrs. Fatz; she was talking about her sister-in-law and something about a cat. I was listening with one ear and was glad when we reached the office. I could tell she was trying to be nice, but…she was *annoying*.

I sat in the main office for a few minutes until a woman in a pinstriped pantsuit came out and introduced herself.

"Good afternoon, Sam, I'm Ms. Rose. Would you like to follow me into my office?"

I nodded and followed the woman into her office. The office was dimly lit, with a love seat, an easy chair with an ottoman, a coffee table, mini fridge, and large mahogany desk.

"Please sit down and make yourself comfortable. Can I get you a drink?" she asked with a pleasant smile on her face.

"No, thanks, I'm good." Although I did take a wad of Kleenex that was on the coffee table and had no problem draining my sinus cavity until it was empty.

Ms. Rose was at her desk looking through a file—probably my file. What did it say? Teen has no parents, lives with aunt and uncle, mediocre student who can't handle life? I was feeling a bit sorry for myself when she looked over at me, got up from her desk, and sat in the chair opposite me on the love seat. She leaned forward with her hands sandwiched together, resting neatly on her knees. She had light brown hair with highlights, shortly cut to her shoulders; she was slender, with newly wrinkled crow's feet in the corner of her eyes. She looked like she may be in her midthirties. She had a calming presence, and she was pretty to look at. I wondered how many overly hormonal boys pretended to *need* "therapy" to be in her presence.

"Sam, would you like to talk about what happened today?" Ms. Rose had her eyes fixed intently on mine.

"Um, well, I guess," I said with as much enthusiasm as going to the *dentist*.

I didn't know where to begin. I didn't even know what happened… Hearing about Sam's loss brought me right back to the sickening feeling of not having any parents, my dad taken from me without any notice, just like mom; well, *she* made a choice to desert her family. I could feel a fresh flood of tears coming. I sat there with my head down, sobbing for an eternity; Ms. Rose didn't say a word. She frequently handed me Kleenex. I was going to have to bring her a new *box*. When I finally looked up, Ms. Rose had her eyes closed, and she was rocking back and forth, looking like she was thinking way too hard.

"Should I go back to class now?" I was feeling even a bit more awkward and wanted to let her know I could see her; she looked a little crazy, and I wanted her to stop.

"Oh, sorry, Sam, I would like to talk to you if you are ready," she said and leaned over and put her hand on mine.

I didn't know what the heck this lady was into, but when she touched my hand, a surge of electricity went through my veins! What was this lady into voodoo?

"Uh, well, is it okay that I am missing class?" *I want to stay, and I want to run—what is with my indecisiveness lately?*

"You are fine to stay, and it is okay if you want to return to class, it's your decision." Ms. Rose gently smiled at me.

"I guess I'll stay." I was a little apprehensive, but I knew there was no way I would be able to concentrate in eleventh-grade English right now.

"What happened today?" Ms. Rose asked again.

"Well, I was in lunch, and my new friend Mariah came in and said that our friend Sam's mother had passed away suddenly," I blurted out with no air in between. I had to catch my breath.

"Oh, I see, yes. Gloire told them in my office this morning. I'm so sorry we didn't call you into the office. I thought they had gotten everyone that was close with Sam."

"Well, I'm not actually close with Sam. I, well, it just reminded me of my dad...and I just lost it," I managed to say without erupting again. *And how the heck does she know Gloire?*

"I thought maybe that was the case, Sam, I am so sorry that you have lost your father. I know this must be so hard for you, so many changes. Of course, this would trigger your emotions."

I was trying to hold back the tears, but they just continued to stream down my face.

"Have you been able to talk about it with any of your friends or your family?" Ms. Rose asked with concern.

Family! Friends! I want to scream! My friends are all back in the city, and my family deserted me! I don't know what to say, but the question enrages me!

"My *friends*…do not live here, and my family is dead and gone! So no…to answer your question, I haven't been able to talk to anyone!" I was surprised by my own response, but Ms. Rose just sat there, peaceful as ever. "Besides, what would talking about it do for me? It's not going to bring anyone back! I can't go back to city and live by myself! I just have to live with this!"

I started shaking and the tears continued to fall. Ms. Rose got up from the chair and returned with a bottled water for me. I took it. She sat back down and waited for me to speak again. I didn't know what to say; I wanted to continue yelling at her for no good reason. She was a stranger trying to help, and all I wanted to do was punish her. What was wrong with me? Where had I gone? I didn't even know who I was anymore.

"Sam, would you like to continue coming here to talk? That's what I am here for. I am here if you need to talk, about anything," Ms. Rose said, looking at me with pity—just what I didn't want, people to feel sorry for me.

I am not sure how long I was in that office, but the dismissal bell rang, and I was headed home. I set up another appointment to see Ms. Rose on Wednesday during my study hall. I also wasn't sure that it did anything to help me, but my options were bleak at this point. My brother was dealing with his grief in his own way, and I just didn't feel comfortable talking about it with Aunt Mimi yet.

When I got home, I went straight to my room, fell on the bed, and slept through the night. I have no idea if someone even tried to wake me. I was so emotionally drained; I did not hear a noise until my buzzer went off at 6:00 a.m. the next morning.

....

Tuesday came and went, and then the dreaded Wednesday was here; another "therapy" session with Ms. Rose and "Amped." *Oh, brother...*

Mariah and Pat had been able to talk to Sam, and they said he was trying to act normal like nothing happened. Sounded like Jake's reaction to my dad passing. I know better than that now. He was going to come to grips with it on his own time and in his own way. Nobody can have an inkling of understanding until they have been through this sort of heartache. That's what it was—heartache. It never seemed to dull, nor did it want to go away. Everything that I see that reminds me of my dad, brings that ache back, a longing that can't and won't be fulfilled. I didn't know Sam well, but I knew that I would be able to understand him on a level that no one else would be able to, not Pat or Mariah.

"See you all at Amped tonight. Remember to bring a card for Sam. We are going to bombard him with our thoughts and prayers!" Mariah said as she hugged our lunch crew good-bye. *I am not looking forward to "church youth group" tonight, neither am I the slightest bit thrilled to be talking about Sam.*

My session with Ms. Rose went a little better today; I was able to talk without being rude, and without sobbing. She really did seem like she actually cared about what I was saying, and she seemed to listen. Once I started talking, it was hard to stop and the time just flew by. Come to find out, she knew Gloire from a youth retreat that the local churches put together for the youth last year. She attended a church outside of Big Run that sometimes got together with other churches in the area for outreach and youth events. Why was everyone in my life now a Jesus-loving freak of some sort? Before I knew it, the bell had rung, and I was on my way home.

After another amazing meal at Aunt Mimi's, we were headed off to youth group. Jake and I sat quietly as Aunt Mimi talked about the pies she was going to bake for the outreach for human trafficking survivors. I had a queasy feeling in my stomach as we approached the little white church. I must have been daydreaming because everyone was out of the car and staring at me.

"Sam, you comin?" Aunt Mimi gave a look of concern outside of the blue Hyundai window.

"Yeah, I'm comin'." My feet felt like lead as we approached the door. *Well, there's no stopping now.*

When Jake and I reached the bottom of the stairs to the youth room, we could hear chanting. The youth were spread out all over the place, each chanting something different from the next. It was bizarre to say the least. Jake and I exchanged glances and had the same idea in mind; if we made a run for it now, no one would even know.

"Hey, guys, thanks for coming," Gloire said from behind as he patted Jake on his back.

"Oh, hey, what's up?" Jake replied quietly as to not disturb the chanting, with his hands resting casually in his pockets.

"As you can see, we are all just spread out, praying for Sam and his family. We would love for you to join in," Gloire said as he moved about the room, chanting like the rest of them.

Jake and I found seats in the back row and sat there in complete silence with our heads down until the chanting came to an end. When the madness stopped, I looked up and Mariah, Pat, and Rachel were sitting next to me.

"I want to thank all you guys for coming tonight and helping our Wednesday service be dedicated to pray for Sam and his family. I was able to see Sam today. He needs your prayers as the celebration service will be held this Friday, here at the church for his mom. If you are able to come, I think that would mean the world to Sam. We have cards on the tables near the coffee bar for you all to sign and give a word of encouragement to Sam. The coffee bar is open. Please don't leave until you have signed one of the cards. Thanks again, and I hope to see many of you on Friday," Gloire said and then his wife Katie turned on some soothing music.

The group disbursed but not in the loud rowdy manner like in Sunday school this past week. I could tell these people really cared about Sam. How can so many youth care about one person so much? Only a couple of my friends came to my dad's funeral. The rest were my dad's co-workers, the little bit of family we had, and other people, I had no clue who they were.

Jake went off with a couple of the boys and was in conversation. Mariah, Pat, and Rachel were sitting around one of the tables at the coffee bar. I must have been staring at them because Rachel motioned for me to come over.

"Sam, come here, we have our own card we want you to sign," Mariah said with sadness in her eyes.

"K, I feel kinda funny 'cuz I don't know him like you guys do," I said as I plopped down into one of the bistro chairs.

"Well, you are part of us now, and Sam will appreciate it," Pat said while staring down at the card, perplexed, I'm assuming, on what to write.

I could feel the warmth reach my cheeks. *I'm part of them?* That made my heart happy.

As the card came into my possession, I stared at it blankly for a minute. What do you say to someone you don't really know, who just lost a parent, when you are going through the same thing, and they don't even know it? Nobody does. I sat for what seemed like an eternity then I wrote:

Sam, I'm not going to say sorry because it doesn't help. I'm not going to tell you it will get better, because that doesn't help either. What I will say is I am here if you want to talk. I am a good listener, and I understand more than you know how much pain you are going through. I'm not real good at praying, but I will try my best and pray that the heartache dulls and you find peace.

Your new friend,
Samantha

I put the card back in the envelope and gave it to Pat. I was hoping that none of them would read what I wrote, but I didn't care too much. I felt I was honest and felt good about what I wrote. Nothing felt worse for me when my dad died, than everyone saying how sorry they were, and that he was in a better place…or that I would see him again someday, or that the heartache would get better. None of that helped even though I knew people were trying to help. No one knows what to say when someone you love is no longer there, but honestly, *sorry* doesn't cut it! And if he is in a better place, that means here with me wasn't good enough, and *if* I see him again someday…when? When will I see him? Right now seems like a good answer.

"Sam, where are you?" Mariah said, looking at me with sincerity.

"Oh, ha, I just spaced out for a minute," I said and realized the whole table was staring at me. Everyone got up from the table, I guess it was time to go, the night had flown by.

Everyone was saying their good-byes and heading up the stairs, when Gloire started walking in my direction.

"Hey, Sam, do you think I could talk to you and Jake for a minute?"

"Uh, yeah sure," I said, searching the room for Jake with my eyes.

Jake caught my eye and headed over to Gloire and me. Mariah and Rachel gave me a hug good-bye and left with Pat.

"What's up?" Jake said and looked back and forth from Gloire to me.

"I just wanted to connect with you two. Would you want to go out for coffee tomorrow night? I can pick you up after dinner. There is a sweet little coffee joint in town where we can chill out and talk," Gloire said, looking at us both with anticipation.

I didn't feel threatened by this youth pastor; he was always laughing, and the group at Amped seemed to really like him. I guess coffee couldn't be so bad.

"Yeah sure, why not," Jake said with a pretty enthusiastic voice.

"Yeah, I have no plans." *I certainly have no plans. I have no life here in Pennsyltucky.*

"Great! I know where your aunt and uncle live. I've been there for an amazing dinner before. I will pick you guys up at 7:00 p.m., is that okay?" Gloire said with a sincere excitement.

"Yeah, that time is perfect," Jake said as Gloire grabbed his hand for a side handshake and pat on the back; he then hugged me good-bye and went on to talk to some other youth that were hanging around.

"See you guys tomorrow night," Gloire shouted in our direction as we headed up the stairs.

I had no idea why this young youth pastor would be so interested in taking two kids to coffee. But he genuinely seemed happy about it. I have never been around a more strange group of people in my life. I missed my friends back in the city, especially Kate. But there was definitely something different about these kids I had so strangely brushed shoulders with here.

5

Change Should Be a Four-Letter Word

After dinner, Gloire came at seven-ish. Aunt Mimi tried to get him to stay for pie, but Gloire thwarted the invite and managed to resist temptation. He had loud rap music blasting in the car and was trying to talk to Jake over the music. *I don't think I'll ever truly understand boys.* As we pulled up to the edge of town, I noticed how cute it actually was. It was clean, and people seemed to be friendly—another difference from the city that was pleasant.

The coffee place was called The One Way Cafe, and it was located in the middle of the town strip. The outside of it had mocha and blue writing on the window, with a sideways coffee cup neon light pouring beans out of the top; it was pretty cool. The perimeter of the interior was neon blue and mocha colored as well, with unique decorations all along the walls. It had little partial wall dividers sectioning off the dining area and each section was designed with a different neon and mocha color. I loved it immediately.

"Hey, Gloire, what is up?" A cute little brunette with smile lines by her eyes came out from behind the counter and yelled as Gloire, Jake, and I walked into the building.

"Hey, Sher, I rounded up a couple more recruits to become addicted to your brew! Ahahaaaaa!" Gloire laughed as they exchanged a huge hug. *Does this dude know everyone! First school, my new friends, the church, now this.*

"Hi, I'm Sheri, nice to meet you two! Welcome to The One Way. I hope you enjoy!"

"Hi, I'm Sam, and this is my brother Jake." We exchanged handshakes then she went back behind the bar.

"What can I get you, guys?" she said with more energy than kids half her age. *Not sure if she needs any more coffee.* "Well, I know no coffee for you, Gloire, let me guess you want an Avalanche. Sam, Jake, what would the two of you like?"

Jake and I ordered lattes, Gloire ordered some sort of organic milkshake called an Avalanche, and then we sat in a section that was neon purple and mocha. The chairs had a silver foundation with gray-covered cushions that had a bouncing coffee beans pattern all over it. There was so much to look at; I don't think I could ever get bored in this place.

Gloire took a giant gulp of his milkshake and said, "Ahhhhhh, there's nothing like a giant Avalanche from this little joint." and then laughed really loud. *I am convinced this man does nothing quietly.*

"Wow, this latte is amazing." I couldn't put it down; the coffee was rich and clean, with the perfect amount of mocha flavoring. It was better than Boulder Café in the city.

"Yeah, not half bad fer round dese parts," Jake said while showing his teeth, then he and Gloire went into a laughing fit.

"So how are you guys adjusting to our mammoth town here?" Gloire said with a wink.

"It's not so bad. I actually like the fact there are so many ball fields. I can't wait to play some baseball next year," Jake said with a look of anticipation.

"Do you play anything else? We play soccer and some b-ball in the elementary school gym on Thursday evenings if you're interested," Gloire said with hopeful eyes.

"Yeah sure, I'll play just about anything when it comes to sports," Jake said with a cockeyed smile.

"What about you, Sam, you into sports at all?" Gloire turned his attention to me.

"Na, I don't really play too many sports. I like to play beach volleyball for fun, but what I really used to love to do is dance." *I haven't said the word dance in over two weeks, boy, do I miss dancing!*

"What do you mean used to love to dance? What made you stop?" Gloire asked innocently.

I wasn't sure how to answer that; I wasn't sure I wanted to answer that question. It would open a whole can of worms I wasn't ready to share with this partial stranger.

"I...uh, well, I used to dance at the School of the Arts in the city. Seeing as the mammoth town as you call it, *Big* Run doesn't have a School of the Arts. I am no longer dancing," I said in a kind of sarcastic tone.

Gloire took another giant gulp of his milkshake and was tapping the straw before he responded. I could feel Jake's eyes beating me down, but I didn't want to look in his direction. I wasn't sure if he had a disapproving look on his face for the way I answered. I had never been this disrespectful to people in my life, and I didn't know where it was coming from.

"Does that mean you have to quit dance altogether?" Gloire asked in a gentle tone.

"No, I don't have to quit, I can do a half of a pirouette in my bedroom, but I am afraid I may break the mirror," I said with a smirk on my face, trying to retract my offensive behavior.

Gloire did half a chuckle, and I quickly glanced at Jake to see if I was in his good graces but he was focused on his latte.

"Ya know, the church has a dance crew that meets every Monday night in the youth room. The dance teacher is a real good friend of mine. When the spirit of God comes on her dancing, it will take your breath away," Gloire said with dancing eyes.

"Oh, that sounds nice," I said casually. *Spirit of God, sounds like some more voodoo crap that I am not about! What is it with these people!*

Halfway through the evening, Gloire's wife, Katie, came in the café. She was always smiling. I was able to get to know her a little bit better. Katie was seven months pregnant with their first child, so sometimes she was not at Amped. Understandably so. She seemed really interested in everything that I had to say. I can honestly say, I haven't run into any other adults that care so deeply about annoying teenagers, as my dad would sometimes jokingly say. All in all, it was a pretty decent night out at the coffee joint. Getting to know these people wasn't half bad. I had never been surrounded by so many caring adults in my life. It was a weird change, but not-bad-at-the-same-time kinda change.

....

Inevitably, the day of the funeral came. Usually on a Friday night, Kate, Mike, and some of our other friends would start out at one of our houses, order pizza, go to the movies, or watch a movie, and we would always end up at Boulder Café. We called it our "usual." It was fun; we always laughed and made some really good memories. Today, I was feeling sorry for myself, and also a bit selfish for wishing I was there right now. Reality was, I was getting ready for a funeral, or however they called it—a celebration service. Which was one of the wackiest titles you can call it when someone has died. How are you to celebrate? I have heard that the Irish have parties at pubs and get smashed. That would go over like a fart in a windstorm in the little white church in Big Run, so I was feeling nervous not knowing what to expect, or how this was going to make me feel. It was just under a month ago; I had to do this for my own father.

Wiping away a few tears, I looked in the mirror and felt a little awkward. I'm used to jeans and T-shirts. I had on black leggings, a long flowing black blouse, chunked high-heel boots, dressed with silver jewelry. The same I wore to my dad's. *Here goes nothing.*

"Sam, Jake, we gotta go," Aunt Mimi yelled from the kitchen.

"Coming!" I yelled back, taking one last glimpse of myself in the mirror.

"Oh, Sam, you are so beautiful, just like your moth…" Aunt Mimi trailed off and looked at me with sad eyes. She is such a sweet woman; I have no idea how her and my *mother* were from the same family.

"Let's go and get this over with," Jake said under his breath but loud enough for us all to hear.

Uncle Joe just looked at Jake, not with eyes of correction, but with eyes of understanding. In spite of our horrible circumstances, Jake and I were lucky to have been welcomed into Aunt Mimi and Uncle Joe's home; who knows where we would be without their love for us. Love, I still have yet to understand. I could feel their genuine care for us, and we really did not know each other all that much. Still, deep down, I knew that I could trust them.

We were greeted at the door of the church by what I presumed to be family members of Sam's. They thanked us for attending and handed us a program with Sam's mother's picture on the front. She was a pretty woman with piercing blue eyes just like Sam's. On the front, it said, "Celebrating the life of Suzanne Cimino." There we were with the celebration stuff again. *How is this a celebration? Isn't that going to offend Sam and his sister? I don't get it. Do these people understand that there is nothing to celebrate when someone dies!?*

We were escorted about halfway down the aisle on the left side and filled up the remainder of the pew. I was on the end and had perfect view of the front. The casket was up front, but it was closed. *Thank God.* There were photos of her all around the front on easels. And then I saw him. He was in the front row on the right side with his head cocked downward.

Sam looked back, and we locked eyes. He wasn't crying, but I could see how red his eyes were even from where I was sitting. People started piling in, and soon, the whole church was full to the point of only standing room in the back of the church. I could not believe how many people there were. *Is everyone from town here?*

The service started out with music, the same kind of music that they played in youth group that they called "worship." The woman singing was smiling from ear to ear with her eyes closed, like she was singing to someone we couldn't see. Her voice was amazing, different from the talent I was used to. She was technically fine, but there was something different about it; I could feel every word that she was singing. People were joining in like we were having church. It was so awkward; I had never been to a funeral like this before. After a few songs, the preacher got up and started to speak.

He talked about Suzanne as if she was alive and well. His message was poised, with appropriate humor about her life and how she had made such and impact on the woman's ministry that she was part of at the church. Not long after, Sam's father, Sam Sr., got up to speak. I was so nervous for him.

After quite a long pause with his head staring down at his paper, Sam Sr. started to speak.

"Good evening everyone. Thank you so much for coming tonight. When talking about if something like this should ever happen to our family, Suzanne expressed that she didn't want a typical wake at a funeral home. She wanted us to share life together, remembering her life with us. So here we are."

Sam Sr. paused, holding back tears and began again. I was holding my own breath, not understanding the strength this man possessed. After a few moments, he began again.

"Never in a million years did I think this day would have come so soon. My selfish side wants her back more than you can imagine. I cannot possibly understand the hand of God. What I do know is that it's on my life, Suzanne's, and on the lives of my children. Suzanne lived life to the fullest and provided an amazing living environment for Sam, Victoria, and me. I am forever thankful for the amazing woman that God blessed me with, and the twenty-plus years that I had the privilege of spending with her. One thing I want to share with you that will help you understand her character is a conversation I had with her not that long ago. Suzanne used her china every day for dinner, and sometimes without fail, one of the kids, or me (he chuckled a bit) would drop a dish, or a bowl, and it would be gone. It always made me nervous watching the kids help their mother setting the table and washing the dishes when we were done. After the last dropping of a dish, I approached Suzanne and asked her, 'Zanny, why do you have to use the china every day? We are constantly replacing broken pieces for your birthday, Mothers' Day, you name it! Why can't we use the not so expensive stuff for every day and use the china for special occasions, like our parents did?'

"Her response to me was so profound, I have since decided to live the rest of my life with this mentality. She said, 'Sammy, my mother never used her china. I can only remember her taking it out a few times in my life when we had "important" guests over for dinner. I remember thinking how wasteful it was having such beautiful plates, bowls, glasses, serving bowls, and dishes, and not using them. They sat in there like it was a museum. I promised myself, if I ever get a beautiful set of china like that, I'm going to enjoy it and use it on the most important people in my life. Well, to me the most important people live with me in my house, I cannot think of anyone person more important than you, Sammy, and our amazing children. If our guests are here to enjoy it with us, then so be it. But I refuse to put items above my family, and teach my children, that they are less important than "company" that we have over for dinner.'

"I was speechless after that conversation, and honestly, it brought me to tears. That moment made me love my wife more than ever before. Thank you and God bless you for being here tonight. Words cannot express my gratitude for the love that you have shown to my family this past week. Please enjoy this next presentation. I have asked Ms. Yvonne to dance to my wife's favorite song."

Sam Sr. got off the stage, and the sanctuary was silent. Next, I saw a woman dressed in a white flowing dance gown standing in second position in front of the sanctuary. The music started, and I recognized the song, it was "I Hope You Dance" by Lee Ann Womack. Ms. Yvonne had shoulder-length curls that bounced happily with every jump. Every movement had purpose; it was soft where it needed to be and fast, and then firm. Each facial expression made the moves stronger. I have danced for eleven years, and I have never seen an adult with the same agility as a teenager. She was amazing, and my heart was so overcome it brought me to tears. They were not tears of sadness, but crazily in the midst of this sad occasion, it made me happy.

The ceremony ended after some more of Suzanne's friends and family spoke, each with special stories and memories of her love and devotion to everyone that was in her life. I am not gonna lie; part of me was jealous of Sam for having such an amazing mother, but that selfishness did not last long when I saw him heading in my direction after we were all dismissed for refreshments in the youth room café.

"Hi, Samantha, thanks for coming," Sam said softly as he approached me. My aunt, uncle, and brother greeted Sam and then walked out of the sanctuary and headed down the stairs.

"Hi," I said with searching eyes. "I can't believe what a beautiful service this was. I have never been to anything like it in my life," I said with as much compassion in my face as I could muster.

"Yeah, my mom was pretty amazing," Sam said, scratching his head and taking in a large breath.

"So how are you doing?" I asked, hoping to not trigger a bunch of emotion that I was not prepared to handle.

"I'm doing okay, I guess, actually I wanted to thank you," Sam said with sad eyes, eyes that had lost some of the twinkle that I was so used to seeing.

"For what?" I was perplexed as to what I could have possibly done to receive a thank-you.

"For what you wrote in the card. I read every response more than once over the past couple of days, and what you said made me feel like you really understood what I was going through. It made me feel not so alone, I guess."

"Um, yeah, you never really know what to say. Sorry just seems not enough, and inaccurate," I said, not really knowing what to say now!

"Yeah, you really did seem to know what to say though," Sam said with a questioning glance.

I wasn't prepared to share, but I felt almost like he deserved an explanation; maybe it would bring some sort of peace. I didn't know, but I felt compelled to share the truth of why I understood.

"Well, actually, Sam, the reason my brother and I just moved here a couple of weeks ago is…well, my father just recently passed away." There I finally said it. I was just hoping for no sympathy.

"I figured something happened. I am sorry that we didn't know about your dad, and that we didn't ask more questions. You are a strong girl to show up to a new school and act the way you do. I only wish we could have been more of a support to you," Sam said with a sincere honesty I wasn't used to seeing in boys my age.

"You couldn't have possibly known unless I told you. I just didn't feel comfortable sharing and then worrying about people feeling sorry for me. And as far as being strong…well, when I found out about your mom, it triggered my emotions, and I kinda lost it at school. I had to spend an entire afternoon in Ms. Rose's office bawling my eyes out. I do want you to know that if you need to talk, I am here, and I definitely understand."

"Thanks, Samantha, that means a lot," Sam said as his attention was turned to the front of the sanctuary where he quickly jogged back to be at his sister's side. She was not handling it well in the present moment as they carried her mother's body out of the sanctuary.

6

Leotards and Lifted Spirits

All through school, Monday, I felt like I was in a partial reality. I was going through the motions, going to class on time, and semi paying attention. My mind was racing with my new life, the new friends, the new home, church, and what I just absolutely could not stop thinking about was that dance at Sam's mom's funeral... celebration service...whatever.

That service made me want to learn more about the strength I had been seeing in the people I was now surrounded by. I started reading a book of the Bible called Esther; it was recommended by Katie, Gloire's wife. She picked out a book that represented seeking God and being strong in our faith. I felt so brand new. It amazed me how strong Esther was, how she risked her life for her people and listened to the words of wisdom that were spoken to her by her uncle. It made me feel kinda pathetic in my reactions to things lately.

I hadn't seen Sam in my morning study hall, so I figured he may be taking another week off school. I wished that I had some more time off after my dad passed to adjust to all this craziness, but as I approached the lunch table, I saw the back of what looked like Sam's tousled hair. As I rested my books and lunch on the large circular lunch table, I noticed Jade sitting across the cafeteria with a bunch of the students who really did not like school. Mariah must have followed my gaze.

"Yeah, Jade has fallen off the face of the earth at least from her friends. I have no idea what happened, but after Peter dumped her, she was out of school for days, and now she won't even talk to us. It's really weird. She hasn't shown up to Amped either," Mariah said with hurt in her voice.

"Wow, I only met her that one time when she saw Peter with that other girl," I said, still gazing in her direction. Jade caught my stare and turned her face while rolling her eyes. She obviously did not want anything to do with this crowd anymore.

My attention quickly turned to Sam, as he caught my questioning gaze, he answered before I asked. "I wasn't in the study hall, kinda got up late. I've just been so tired. I gotta get back into the swing of things here," he said, looking back down at his food, willing himself to eat.

"Well, if anyone has an excuse to be tired, bud, it's you. Take it easy and let us know if you need anything. Really, I mean it. Don't push yourself too much," Pat said while patting his back.

Sam didn't look up, I knew the feeling. Not wanting to eat, or talk, or be around people who had no clue what I was going through. It was exhausting.

"I have to ask a question about something. Have any of you ever been to the dance class on Mondays?" I blurted out rather quickly.

Mariah, Rachel, Pat, and Sam all looked up at me.

"No, I haven't, I would scare everyone with my not-so-catlike reflexes. Rachel said as she sucked in her face and tried to do a ballerina pose.

The group let out a chuckle.

"Why do you ask, Sam?" Mariah asked.

"Well, I used to attend the School of the Arts in NYC, and I am kinda missing my dance classes and performances." Hoping I would be enlightened on Ms. Yvonne and her dance class I watched for all responses.

"Well, I know for a fact that Ms. Yvonne is looking for someone to replace Jade. She quit dance as well, and they go to fine arts competition every year. I know that Ms. Yvonne was depending on Jade. It's so sad that she has dropped out of everything," Mariah said with sad but hopeful eyes.

"Oh, I'm not so sure about competition, but I would love to be able to dance again. Do you think she would mind if I went to check it out?"

"For sure! I know she would be thrilled, especially if you have a strong background in dance," Mariah said with a smile from ear to ear.

"Well, I guess it's worth checking out!" I said with just as much enthusiasm. It was the first time in weeks that I had a twinge of excitement. The rest of the school day could not go any faster. I was hoping that Aunt Mimi would allow me to go and give me a ride. I was pretty sure she would be happy to do just that.

It was an easy sell to Aunt Mimi; she frantically made an early dinner just so I could sit down as a family and eat with them. Dance class started at 6:00 p.m. and I didn't want to be late, especially since they had no idea I was coming. I figured it was worth a shot to at least go and check it out. I had my bag ready to go and went to the fridge to get a water bottle and piece of fruit. Aunt Mimi was watching me with a smile from ear to ear.

"Why are you smiling so big, Aunt Mimi?" I asked with a similar expression; it was hard to be anything but happy around my aunt.

"You feel comfortable here. That is the first time you went to the fridge and got something out without asking. You have no idea how happy that makes me." Aunt Mimi looked as if she wanted to cry.

"Oh, ha, I guess I didn't even think about it," I said and I could feel my cheeks turn a bit of red.

"Yes, that's right. You didn't even have to think about it. I have been praying that you would see this as your home, feeling comfortable with the house, with me and your uncle. Sam, I am so happy that you and Jake decided to let Uncle Joe and I make a home for you. We don't have a lot, but what we do have is yours." Aunt Mimi was reaching in for a hug, and I let her.

"Thank you, Aunt Mimi. Jake and I do feel comfortable here. You have made this transition the best you possibly could have for us under the circumstances. And we do both appreciate everything that you have sacrificed for us," I said with just as much sincerity, and now I want to cry!

"This has been anything but a sacrifice. You and Jake are an added blessing in our lives. More than you could possibly know," Aunt Mimi said while she put on a light jacket and got the keys to the car.

The familiarity of the youth room calmed my nerves a bit. There were six dancers on the dance floor stretching, while others were trickling in and heading to the bathroom, probably to change. I came prepared with my leotard on. All I had to do was strip down and put on my shoes. *If I was welcomed to participate.* It was 5:50 p.m., and Ms. Yvonne was nowhere in sight. The range of dance gear was bewildering. Some had on very exquisite dance apparel while others where in sweats, but everyone had on ballet slippers.

"Sorry everyone! My husband got home late, and I had dinner on the stove—yada, yada, yada!" Ms. Yvonne came barreling down the stairs as fast as she could. She had two large bags that she quickly threw to the side. She took off her sweat pants and shirt and was fully dressed in dance wear ready to go. "Okay everyone please take a seat on the dance floor. I have some announcements." She then stood at the front of the dance floor with her hands folded, smiling while she patiently watched everyone take a place on the floor.

Everyone proceeded to stop what they were doing and followed directions. I put down my bag and quickly scooted to the back of the dance floor, hoping not to make a spectacle of myself. As I plopped myself down, two girls next to me gave me a cockeyed glance with a half smirk and then turned their attention back on Ms. Yvonne.

As I turned my gaze forward, I locked eyes with Ms. Yvonne, and she raised her eye brows upward while still smiling. It was a welcoming look. *Phew, I do not want to be a distraction to what she is doing.*

"Okay, as you all know, we are starting to prepare for State Fine Arts Competition. I will need to know by November 1 who is going to participate this year. We will still be ministering at the church with our dance, as well as the various outreaches throughout the year. If you do decide to compete, you are committing to doing the outreaches. We believe that God gave us our talents, and although competition is fun, it isn't the only reason we do what we do. God has given us gifts to share with the world, so we will dance for God with all our might! Please see me after class if you want the paperwork for competition. Remember if you are competing, you are also committing to extra dance practices. Okay, now, please everyone at the bar for warm-ups."

Everyone took a place on the bar; I made sure that I was all the way in the back. Ms. Yvonne prayed over us for protection and His…spirit? Then she put on some soft music and everyone started going through the dance positions, plié, and following through with lines. There was a large display of beginners all the way to intermediate. There were a couple of girls that had amazing feet and a dream of a dancer's body. I was nervous; I hadn't danced in almost a month. My body seemed to adjust rather quickly; it felt good going into all the positions, stretching my muscles, and following through with my arm extensions. Slowly, Ms. Yvonne was making her way down the line, watching each dancer, pushing on stomachs, straightening arms, guiding the turnout. She made her way to me and stopped. She had on a big smile and asked, "Hi, I'm not sure we have met, I'm Ms. Yvonne, how did you hear about The Dance Crew?"

"Um, hi, I'm Sam, and I'm sorry to just show up like this, but Gloire mentioned it, and then I was talking with Mariah, and she said it would be okay to just show up, and by the way, your dance at the funeral... celebration service...well, it was breathtaking, so I figured that I would come by, and I hope this is okay," I said like a rollercoaster with no brakes.

"It's more than fine, and I am glad that you enjoyed the dance. God was really helping me hold it together. Suzanne was a dear friend of mine." Ms. Yvonne said with sad eyes.

"Oh, great! I mean, great, it's okay, I'm here. It's been almost a month since I've been able to dance, and I have been craving leotards, slippers, and a hard wood floor." I was elated that I was welcome to be here.

"From the look of your turnout, arm extensions, and positioning, I would say that this is more than a hobby?" Ms. Yvonne asked with a warm smile.

"Yeah, I used to attend the School of the Arts, in NYC, until I moved here." I said, hoping not to have to get into my depressing story.

"Well, let's see whatcha got, and I will have a better feel as to what group to put you in," Ms. Yvonne said and walked back to the front of the dance floor.

"Okay everyone, we are going to do a three step amalgamation, start in third position, and move into a chasse, then pirouette into an arabesque. Please line up, Princess group first, then Ladies, and lastly Queens."

The group lined up, most of the group measured not in just talent, but in age as well. There were only a few older girls that lined up in the Princess or Ladies group. I wasn't sure where I should go, so I stood off to the side. Ms. Yvonne gently guided me to the back of the line next to the Queens. I was getting nervous, knowing that I hadn't practiced in so long. The Princess group went first, and there were a couple of girls that were going to be amazing in a few years. The Ladies group was very much evenly disbursed in the range of talent. When it became time for the Queens, my stomach started doing flip-flops.

The two girls who gave me a half smirk in the beginning of class were beautiful and talented. I wasn't quite sure how to take their attitudes. I wasn't sure if they were genuine or not. My turn came, and my heart was beating out of my chest. I started in third, rounded out my arms, went in for the chasse with appropriate speed, did an elevated pirouette, and landed into a perfect-angled arabesque. It felt sooo good! I turned around just in time to see the two girls look at each other with scowls on their faces. I could see that they were not going to be welcoming me here. I didn't care. I missed the feeling of freedom that dance gave me, and if Ms. Yvonne wanted me here, I would stay as long as I could. The rest of the dance practice we learned a small routine that Ms. Yvonne wanted the entire group to learn. It was an easy routine, but done as a group looked beautiful. I did not want practice to end.

When practice was over, parents flooded the room, dance bags were everywhere, and people were waiting in line to talk to Ms. Yvonne. I finished getting my stuff together and was about to head up the stairs to meet Aunt Mimi when I felt a tug at my jacket.

"Where are you going off to so quickly?" Ms. Yvonne said as I turned around to face her.

"Oh, ha, I think my aunt is waiting upstairs, thank you so much for letting me come. You have no idea how good that felt."

"It is my pleasure. Sam, do you want to continue coming? I…we would love to have you. From what I've seen today, you have some real talent, and matched with the love of dance, you have potential to really go somewhere with your dancing. I would love the opportunity to teach you what I can," Ms. Yvonne said with prancing eyes.

"Really? Yes! I will be here every week. Thank you for your kind words."

"I would really like to talk to you about the fine arts program also. Would you be interested in taking extra classes to learn special dances to be in competition?" Ms. Yvonne had a serious look on her face; she wasn't kidding.

"I would love to take extra classes. I am not sure how much we can afford, though. I would have to talk to my aunt before I give you a definite answer." I couldn't make a decision when it came to money. I had no idea what my aunt and uncle could pay for.

"Oh, nonsense, this is the ministry that God gave me, the youth that are here do not pay for classes. You only have to pay for state and national competition, and we have fundraisers to offset some of the costs of competition. So what do you say?"

"Really? Wow, well then, of course! I would love to spend as much time as possible dancing."

"Well then, it's settled! I have a spot at 5:00 p.m. on Mondays that just recently opened up. One of my main dancers just quit out of nowhere. So if you could come one hour before practice on Mondays, we can get started next week!" Ms. Yvonne said while looking through her planner. It was odd seeing someone use an actual planner that you had to write in and not use and iPod or iPad, or some other electronic device.

"Great! And thanks again. I'll see you next week, or maybe Sunday at church." I was so ecstatic that I was dancing again. I felt a tiny twinge bad knowing that I was probably taking Jade's spot. But that didn't last long. *Besides, she chose to quit!*

The next few days were filled with homework, eating more fantastic dinners by Aunt Mimi, and getting used to my new friends. I was feeling so comfortable to the point where I finally was able to show my silly side. During lunch on Wednesday, Mariah was talking about a fundraiser they were doing for the church, and when she looked at me, I had put my lips up to the point of only my teeth showing when I answered her question; and Sam, Pat, and Rachel died of laughter, while Mariah was just staring at me. Then she proceeded to talk in a helium-filled-sounding voice, which made me spit my water clear across the table, spraying Pat and Sam in the process. After the initial shock of being spit upon, Pat, Sam, Rachel, Mariah, and I were laughing so hard the entire lunchroom took notice. I was feeling so much better about my life here in Big Run.

As I was leaving the counselor's office from my regular Wednesday appointment with Ms. Rose, I ran into Sam on the way out. He gave me a quick smile, a two-finger salute, and a knowing look. Normally I would have been embarrassed being seen coming out of a counselor's office, but with Sam, it was different. He and I were in the same boat, and it was actually soothing knowing someone else understood exactly how I felt.

During Amped on Wednesday, I noticed I was actually able to sing along with some of the songs. I also noticed for the first time how beautiful Mariah's voice was; she was able to pick out all the harmonies and sound amazing with every note. Mariah was also competing in fine arts competition for singing. We would be traveling together when the time came! I still couldn't believe I was going to be competing in dance again; a newfound desire to dance forced me to move my furniture around in my room, so I had some sort of space to practice. Lately I could not stop dancing.

Back to reality, Sam was next to me, and he was raising his hands and singing and swaying to the music. I could not figure out why he was feeling so much better so quickly, it had only been a week and a half since his mom passed. Crazy. I could not figure out a lot about these people, but one thing that was undeniable, they were my friends; I knew they cared about me, and I had never known people my age to be so real.

"Young people, press in! Keep pushing, God is here! He wants to know you more, give Him your whole heart, He will never fail you. God, please be the center of our lives! We give You all the glory, honor, and praise.

I feel in my spirit that there are people here who want to give their lives to God. If you feel a stirring in your spirit, come up here and I will pray with you, please don't hesitate. God is calling you. All you have to do is answer Him. He will meet you where you're at."

After Gloire's heart cry, I felt a throbbing in my heart that would not go away. I had no idea what it was, but I felt compelled to go forward. I had my head down and my eyes semi-closed, and I was willing this crazy heartbeat to go away but it wouldn't. When I finally opened my eyes, I saw a familiar figure up in the front on his knees with his hands in the air. It was Jake. I rushed over to him, fell on the floor, and buried my face in his side. We held each other and cried. There was so much emotion going through my veins I started to tremble. Gloire and his wife Katie came and fell on the ground beside us, praying in weird voices. I didn't care. I was feeling something that I had never felt before, and I did not care who saw. Then Gloire started to pray in between sobs.

"God, I thank you for these two precious young people that you have brought to us. I thank you for their lives. I thank you for your Son that you sent to die on the cross to forgive us of our sins. God, we repent for our unholiness. God, we ask that you would mend our brokenness. God, I ask that you would show them how much you love them and how much you want to be their daddy. God, I pray that you would show Sam how beautiful she is to you, how much you cherish her. Sam, God smiles when you dance, He cherishes you, He loves you, He is proud of you. Jake, God says that you are a young man of integrity, and He is going to use you to speak to others, to bring encouragement, and to show them who God is. I need you two to repeat this after me, if you believe that Jesus is God's son, that He died on the cross to save you, and if you want to have a relationship with Him."

Both Jake and I nodded; we really didn't understand too much, but this feeling inside of us would not go away, and it just felt right.

"Dear God, I ask you to come into my heart, forgive me of my sins, and be the Ruler of my life. I know that Jesus is your son, and he died to save me so I can be reunited with you forever. I thank you for my life, in Jesus's name, amen."

After we all repeated what Gloire said, I opened my eyes and was greeted with tear-stained faces from Gloire, Katie, Jake, and behind me was Mariah, Rachel, Pat, Sam, and a couple of Jake's friends. The moment was indescribable; for the first time in a very long time, I felt peace.

7

Old and New Collide

October flew by with my new dance classes, getting to know Mariah and the crew, weekend sleepovers with Mariah and Rachel, "coffee chats" with Gloire, Jake, and Katie at The One Way Cafe, performing a group dance for the fall human trafficking outreach (through which we raised over $5,000 for a local organization that helps women and children who have been directly affected!), and major school work in preparation for the end of the quarter. My life seemed crazy at times with all the new things that I was involved with. I was slowly getting into the groove here at my Aunt and Uncle Joe's as well. Jake was getting close to Uncle Joe; he helped Uncle Joe fix the porch and put up a new swing for Aunt Mimi's fifty-third (which, of course, brought her to tears). Jake and I were definitely on the mend. We missed Dad every day, but we were able to talk about him so much more, without the feeling of complete misery. At times I missed New York, but I was really enjoying being surrounded by nature. It was beautiful and the changing of the seasons was a magical time when you could see all the beauty in God's creation.

I was learning so much about the Bible from Gloire and Katie, *who, by the way, looks like she is going to pop!* They met with us weekly, discussing our sin nature and how we all needed to be reconciled with God the father, and how He has love for every child that He created. It was mind blowing when I thought about eternity. I just couldn't get out of my head how that worked just yet. How could we live forever? I guess our pea-brained skulls would not ever be able to understand it, that's where faith comes in. Well, at least that is what I'm learning. I was new to all of this, but I had such a peace in my spirit, even more so than before my dad passed. It was undeniable to me that there was a God now. I still do not know why my dad was taken so early, but I had peace that God loved me. He loved my dad, and my brother. The pounding in my heart told me so.

The start of November brought on the cold weather like it was timed. It was difficult going through my bins of winter clothes, outfits that my dad had bought me, or had given me money to go shopping. Tears fell with almost every article of clothing as I hung them up or folded them and put them away. My dad would be so proud of the way I was keeping my room clean. I started off here with a clean room, and *I have managed to keep it that way for almost a month and a half!*

As the first Friday in November came to an end, I had a moment of reflection on the bus ride home from school. These past several weeks, my life had changed so drastically. I was thankful that I was not new to the school anymore; it was nice to have a settled stomach with each passing day. I was actually enjoying the school and, of course, my new friends. Sam and I had gotten together a couple of times after school at The One Way Café to talk. He was doing so good; he was actually helping me cope I think more than I was helping him. His dad was remarkable and so strong. His little sister Victoria was taking it the worst. At the end of our conversations, we would always pray for her.

Uncle Joe was in town waiting for Jake and me to take us home. He stopped by the bakery and bought two loaves of Italian bread. *What? Aunt Mimi isn't making her own bread for dinner, and two loaves?* It was definitely questionable. When we got back to the house, Aunt Mimi was waiting in the doorway with the front door open and only the screen door in front of her, with a huge smile on her face, similar to the day we arrived. I thought this was rather odd; it was only about fifty degrees outside, and she was always so insistent on not heating the outdoors. Jake and I walked up the steps and Aunt Mimi opened the door.

"Surprise!" Out jumped Kate and Jake's best friend, Brad, from New York.

The next few minutes were filled with tears of happiness and bear hugs and kisses, from Kate and me of course. Jake and Brad were laughing as Jake kept saying, "Holy crap, I can't believe you're here." Uncle Joe stood by with a grin from ear to ear, and Aunt Mimi had her hands on her cheeks with tears flowing down the sides of her face. I ran over to her and hugged her like never before and planted a huge kiss on her forehead. Jake followed suit and gave her a big hug, then we bombarded Uncle Joe with hugs as well.

"We wanted to surprise you with your friends. They are here for the weekend! We know how hard this has been on the both of you. We have a delicious dinner of stuffed chicken breasts, loaded baked potatoes, and corn on the cob. Then we are dropping all of you guys off in town for a movie and drinks at The One Way. Sound good?" Aunt Mimi said as if she had just given us a million bucks. Well, she may as well have, 'cuz this felt like a million bucks.

"Oh my gosh, Aunt Mimi, Uncle Joe, thank you so much! I don't even know what to say!" I was so overcome with emotion the tears just started to fall.

"Oh, Sam, get yourself together. We need to catch up!" And with that, Kate slapped me in the back, just like old times. It felt good.

"Yeah, thanks so much, I am completely shocked!" Jake said as he high-fived Brad.

"Go ahead and catch up. We will eat in about an hour and then we will drop you guys off for your night on the town!" Aunt Mimi said and then started back in the kitchen. Uncle Joe went to his favorite chair and pulled out the newspaper and started reading from the front with his legs crossed over, resting on the ottoman.

When I got to my room, the surprise was not over. There was big blow-up mattress all made with a complete sheet and comforter set. There was a card on the bed with my name on it. I quickly opened it up while Kate took out her stylish New York clothes and started hanging them on hangers. The card had two movie tickets for the little theater in town, and a

$15 gift card to The One Way. I just could not believe how thoughtful my aunt was. I ran out of the room and hugged her tightly from behind while she was preparing the potatoes in front of the stove.

"Thank you so much, you went above and beyond," I said, trying not to cry again.

"You know, it was your uncle's idea to get you the gift cards," Aunt Mimi said, returning my hug. "And you are so welcome," she said as she kissed my forehead.

I went over to Uncle Joe and kissed him, too, on the forehead and smiled. He smiled back and waved his hand over his head. His cheeks flushed crimson. He was a man of few words, but his heart said many.

As I headed back to my room, I ran into Jake in the wood-paneled hallway.

"Dude, what the freak! I can't believe they set this whole thing up!" he had a similar card in his hands, and I presumed he was on his way to do the same thing I had just done.

"I know, this is unbelievable," I said as I walked into my room to see Kate swaying to the beat of a Taylor Swift song "Shake It Off."

"Gurrrl, get your butt over here and dance! Oh, oh, oh, shake it off." Kate grabbed me by the hands and was shaking me back and forth so violently that I couldn't catch my breath. We both fell over onto the air mattress and started laughing our butts off.

"I can't believe you are actually here! Oh my gosh, where have you been all my life!" I didn't realize until now how much I missed Kate's boisterous personality. She was never nervous about anything. I envied her charisma and ability to take change so easily.

"Ahhhh, girl, where do I start? I miss your face so much at school!" Kate sat up abruptly. "Do you remember James, the guy you had a crush on last year? The one from our drama class? He is dating Joley's little sister Ashley! She is a freshman! These boys and their young appetites…ugh! And oh my goodness."

Kate went on to tell me all the gossip at the School of the Arts; she told me about her new classes, the new competition. In that school, the better you were, the more opportunities came your way. Kate was a musician and a drama student. There were a few new students who transferred from other schools that had major talent. Kate was nervous that they were going to outdo her in the talent showcase at the end of the year. I, of course, reassured her of how great she was, which she really was in fact an amazing actress and singer/song writer, and then she, of course, went on to tell me her woes of her relationship with Mike Shuller. Which was nonexistent as of last Friday. She was on to new and better things. I cuddled a hot cup of tea while listening to Kate; I think I could have sat on that air mattress, sipped tea, and listened to Kate all day. It was familiar. It was good.

After dinner, Uncle Joe dropped us off in front of the little theater just as promised. We all decided to see the new *Hunger Games* movie, *Mockingjay*; it had just been released to theaters and we had all read the trilogy. Jake and I saw quite a few students from school, and it was nice to be remembered. Kate winked at me when any male person nodded or said hi to me. She was ridiculous as always, eyeing every boy that came her way.

The movie was epic! We walked the short distance to The One Way while discussing any differences that we noticed from the book.

"This little joint has a feel of the city!" Kate said as we approached the coffee shop.

"I know, I think I'm pretty much addicted to the almond joy lattes," I said as we all approached the counter.

"Hello, Jake and Sam, what can I get you, guys?" Sheri, the owner of the coffee shop had gotten to know Jake and me by first names. Needless to say, we were in here quite a bit.

"Hey, Ms. Sheri, I'll have the usual. Kate, what would you like?" Jake was pointing out the different drinks to Brad and describing it, like he was a barista.

"Oh, geez, um, well, I'll have an Americano with an extra shot of espresso, and a shot of toffee nut. Kate always ordered something different every time we went to Boulder in the city. She loved trying new things. I wished sometimes I could be more adventurous, but I always ended up ordering the same thing! I just didn't want to be disappointed; I liked what I liked and that was that.

"Sam! Hey, toots, what are you up to? I tried calling your house. Aunt Millie said you were out. I was like, what? Is she on a date and didn't tell me?!" Mariah had her arms around my neck and didn't notice Kate until Kate introduced herself.

"Hi, I'm Kate, Sam's friend from the city," Kate said, extending her hand. Kate had straight blond hair; she was tall, thin, with legs for days. It was hard *not* to notice Kate.

"Oh, hi! I'm Mariah, that's so nice you came to visit. What are you lovely ladies up to tonight? Rachel and Sam are meeting me here, can we join?"

I could see the look on Kate's face; it was friendly, but I could tell she was a little disheartened. I mean, really, we hadn't seen each other in almost two months. I didn't want to upset her, but I didn't want to leave Mariah out either. I felt stuck. Before I could answer, Sam and Rachel walked in. They saw all of us and nodded, heading in our direction. Jake and Brad were whispering and looking from Mariah, to Rachel, to Kate—oh brother literally, teen boys and their hormones.

"Fancy meeting you here!" Rachel said, doing her goofy ballet pose again. She was a trip.

"Hey, you guys just get here?" Sam said as he took notice of Kate and Brad. "Hey, guys, I'm Sam, not sure I've seen you two around here before."

His attention was mostly focused on Kate. Her hair was always shiny and long and flowing; she had on long high-heeled boots, shiny leggings, a multicolored long-fitted Chenille sweater, and jewelry to match. She definitely stuck out in Big Run.

"Oh, honey, that's because we are not from here. We are friends from the city, but it is a pleasure to meet you," Kate said, flashing Sam a flirty smile. I wasn't sure how I felt about that; I wasn't interested in a romantic relationship with Sam, but I definitely wasn't ready to set him up with my best friend either.

Sam blushed. "Nice to meet you too, ha. Well, shall we order?" His attention quickly turned back to Mariah and Rachel.

They made their way to the front of the counter. Kate, Brad, Jake, and I went to the Audrey Hepburn section of the shop. It was neon blue and mocha, with black and white artwork and paintings of Audrey Hepburn. The section had a huge sign that said "Breakfast at Tiffany's." Kate was right; this definitely did have a city feel to it. Maybe that was one of the reasons I was so drawn to it. After Sam, Mariah, and Rachel got their drinks, they headed over to our section, pulled up a table, and sat down. Kate no longer looked upset. I think she was happy to have Sam to flirt with.

I was amazed at how my old friends and new friends made a possible uncomfortable situation comfortable. Mariah and Rachel were firing questions to Brad and Kate on city living. They were all so interested in how the "rest of the world" lived, as Sam put it. Kate was ecstatic to have so much attention, and I was just happy that everyone was getting along. It was nice to sit back and listen; every now and then, Jake and I would add some interesting facts about city life. It was our not so-long-ago past, which felt as if it was eons prior to life in Big Run and Punxsutawney. Time ran away from us, and soon, the shop closed and Uncle Joe was waiting patiently for us outside of the coffee shop.

Kate and I stayed up half the night, talking about school, friends, our NYC adventures; it was timeless, I missed her crazy self, and I realized I used to rely on her so much for affirmation and stepping out and trying new things. Having to move into a new town, away from everyone that I knew and loved, made me have to learn how to step out on my own…maybe for the first time.

I could smell the bacon and eggs, waffles, and potatoes. It woke me up from a sound sleep. I stretched and sat up, expecting Kate to be lying on her stomach with the blankets everywhere, but she was nowhere to be seen.

Kate was in the kitchen sipping coffee, talking nonstop to Aunt Millie who was busy at the stove, making sure all the meal components were done at the same time. I had no idea how she managed to do that, but I was determined to learn at least that while I was here!

"Well, look who finally got herself out of bed!" Kate said while shifting her head back and forth.

"Yeah, what the heck? You are always the last one up!" I said while giving her pony a tug.

"Girl, please, it's 11:00 a.m.! We have limited time, and I want to squeeze out every ounce of time I have left with you!" Kate said as her eyes got wide with anticipation as my aunt set the food down on the table. "Oh, Aunt Millie, I would be seven hundred pounds if I ate like this every day! But for today, I'm going to feast!" Kate said as she didn't hesitate to start piling her plate with food.

Not more than two minutes later, Jake and Brad joined the table for breakfast. I think it was Aunt Mimi's way of getting us up! No one could resist the smell of her home-cooked anything.

After breakfast—well, brunch—Jake and Brad settled in the living room still in pajamas playing Brad's new PlayStation 4. I'm sure no matter what Kate and I decided to do for the day, we would return to find Brad and Jake in the same position. Kate and I showered and slowly got ready for the day and decided to take a walk. Kate kept commenting on how she had never seen so many trees and leaves changing color. I realized I had not even ventured out to explore my aunt and uncle's neighborhood. They didn't have "neighbors" close to the house. My aunt said that in the opposite direction of town, there wasn't another house for about a mile down the road! Unheard of in the city.

"Ahhhh, I just love the country air here! Can you smell that? It's the smell of no pollution!" Kate said as she linked her arm through mine.

"I know, although I love the different smells of the city, like the fresh baked rolls, the smell of freshly brewed coffee, food from the street vendors, I also love the smell of the air here in Big Run…the air is definitely different here! I was told I would not love the smell as much during fertilizing season," I said as I plugged my nose while I spoke. Kate chuckled.

"So tell me, what is up with that boy named Sam?" Kate asked very coyly.

"What do you mean, what is up with him?" I asked, feeling my cheeks getting warm.

"He is not hard to look at, *Sam*, and he definitely has his attention on you!" Kate said, looking at me like I was hiding something. I stopped walking and turned to face Kate.

"Really, Kate, there is nothing *up* with him. Honestly. We have connected, but not like you are thinking. Sam just recently lost his mother. We have been talking and sharing with each other because we understand like no one else can." I could see the hurt in

Kate's eyes, knowing that she could not be there for me, like she would be if I were closer.

"Oh, wow, I didn't realize. I'm so sorry, Sam. I am sorry I haven't brought it up. I do want to know how you are doing. I can't even imagine what this has been like for you, and I hate the fact that you no longer have your cell phone!" Kate said while punching the air in front of her.

"I know, it was really tough in the beginning. I have met some pretty cool people, though. I have been blessed with some great new friends and a church that has really welcomed me and my brother in." I noticed Kate's confused expression as I mentioned the word "blessed" and "church."

"Wait, hold up… *Church*? You? You always used to laugh at me when my parents made me go on Easter and Christmas! Now you're blessed? What is going on? Ahahaha, I can't even picture you sitting in church and chanting," Kate said, amusing herself with the thought.

"Well, picture it. I honestly would not be as far as I am right now without the peace that I felt ever since I met these people, and…ever since I…um, well, I accepted Jesus in my heart," I said, not really wanting to hear Kate's response.

"You're actually serious about this! Oh, wow, um, hahaha. Sorry to laugh, it's just a bit to process, that's all. Accepted *Jesus* in your heart? What exactly does that mean?" Kate said while looking at me perplexed. *Do I even know what I am talking about?*

"I don't want to confuse you with my words. It just means that I believe that God sent His son Jesus to the world, to live like us, and then He died so that our sins could be forgiven, and we will someday be with Him in heaven. Does that make any sense?" I asked, hoping not to confuse her even more. I was new to all this stuff, and if anyone would have told me I would be saying this a month ago...*you might have gotten a fist in the face!*

"Yeah, I've heard the same type of thing from one of the kids at school who is constantly trying to get me to go to her church...and I have heard some stuff when we go on holidays...but I never thought you would actually believe any of it! I'm not judging, just saying, if it works for you, great!" Kate said with unbelieving body language.

"Well, I do believe it, because I felt it. It wasn't just a decision I made. I am telling you, Jake and I both felt it, it was like we were being pulled or something," I said, looking ahead as we were approaching the first signs of life. We must have walked at least a mile already because there was my aunt and uncle's "neighbor's" house. *Geez, I guess you could never go next door to borrow anything!*

"Whoa, whoa, whoa, just stop. Jake too? Okay, okay, I get it you guys have been through a lot. We will just keep it at that.... Wow, check out the log cabin! I really did not think people actually lived like this anymore. Although that's a pretty nice log cabin."

I was happy to divert the attention to something else. I could tell that Kate was just not going to understand what I was talking about; she was going to have to experience it on her own. The log cabin was huge! The house had a full wraparound porch with lights wrapping the posts that held the roof of the porch in place. There were Adirondack chairs and rocking chairs lined up with little coffee tables in between each set, going the distance of the massive porch. My aunt would be in her glory with this porch. There was a barn to the right of the house, and just as we approached center viewing, a girl holding the bridal of a horse came walking out of the barn. She had long black hair and stopped suddenly when she saw us. It was Jade.

"Hi, Jade, is that you?" I asked, acting like I wasn't sure that it was her. She proceeded to walk closer. It was definitely Jade; the one who suddenly stopped talking to all of her friends, quit dance, and stopped church all together. The one whom I replaced.

"Yeah, uh, hey, what are you doing here?" She asked with a puzzled look on her face.

"I live with Millie and Joe Anderson," I said, not knowing if she would remember.

"Oh yeah, I forgot about that, haha. Um, well, nice to see you," she said, kind of awkwardly, returning her attention to the massive horse she was walking.

"She is beautiful. I mean, is it a she?" The horse was brown with white lining the forehead and white hoofs.

"Oh yes, meet Cassy, she is six years old and loves to be pet," Jade said while petting the bridge of the snout of the magnificent animal.

"Wow, I can't say I've seen a horse up that close before! Well, besides the police horses they have patrolling the streets in the city," Kate said while giving Cassy a pet on the side of her head.

"Oh, geez, I'm so sorry, Jade, this is Kate. She is my best friend from the city. Kate, this is Jade, she goes to my school." *I am bad at introductions.*

"Hi, your house is sick! I mean, wow! It looks like it belongs on the cover of a magazine!" Kate said as she stared at the house in awe.

"Oh, ha, thanks, my father built it five years ago. My papa passed away and left quite a large inheritance. So my dad built my mom the home of her dreams," Jade said, smiling at first and then her smile faded. "Um, do you want to come in? I can show you around if you would like," Jade asked with sincerity.

I was definitely down to see the inside of this house! It was gorgeous!

"Um, heck yeah! You can count me in. Do you mind if I take some pics with my phone? I gotta show the kids back in the city the way county folk live it up!" Kate said while taking a selfie with the house in the background without waiting for a response from Jade. Jade and I busted out laughing. It was good to see Jade without the eye rolling. She seemed so much different than how she had been acting in school. I never got a chance to know her, but I do know that Mariah and Rachel missed her like crazy. I was definitely on a mission to see if I could find anything out.

The inside was just as gorgeous as the outside. The great room, as they called it, had a ceiling that went as high as the roof. There was a giant sky window over the room. The furniture was that of a modern, rustic look. The upstairs had a loft that overlooked the great room. The dining room opened up into the living room, and the kitchen opened up into the dining room. The whole place was open and had the feel of a high-end lodge. It was beautiful and the craftsmanship throughout the whole house was meticulous, every detail was thought out. Jade's room was gorgeous. It was huge! She had a large sleigh bed at least queen size, and furniture to match. She had her own bathroom with a large Whirlpool tub and separate shower. I could not imagine what the master bedroom looked like! Her room was upstairs and shared the middle section, the loft, with her younger sister. The loft area had a couch and table with a large flat panel television. It was protected with a large wooden banister that went the length of the loft area. There were beautiful carvings in the wood throughout the entire house.

"How long did it take to build this house?" I asked in utter bewilderment.

"It was a long process. My dad is a writer, so he was able to do both at the same time. It took four years to build. We just moved in last year." Our old house is farther back in the property. We kept it up for company or the church has used it in the past when guest speakers come in from out of town." Jade trailed off and went somewhere else in her head as she mentioned church.

Kate was looking at everything and taking tons of pictures. I couldn't help but see the look of pain in Jade's expression. *What the heck is going on?* I wanted to know, but I was afraid to ask. I mean, we definitely weren't friends—not yet, at least.

"Jade, can I ask you something?" I said, looking at her in a serious gaze.

"Sure. What's up?" Jade was looking down at the ground with her hands pushing down hard in her pockets.

"I…we…ya know, Mariah, Rachel, and the guys… well, we are wondering why you left the table, and well, Amped and stuff." Man, did I sound like an idiot.

Jade looked over the loft, and just as she was about to speak, the giant front doors to the log house opened up wide.

"Jade! Come help with the groceries please…ugh, my arms are going to fall off! Hahaha, they had quite the deals at Super Walmart in Punx. Got your favorite cereal!" The black-haired woman had long flowing hair just like Jade.

"Coming, Mom," Jade said with not so much enthusiasm. "Do you guys want to come meet my mom?" Jade asked but didn't leave room for an answer before she started down the stairs. Kate and I followed.

"Oh, hi, I didn't know we had guests!" Jade's mom plopped four large bags of groceries on the massive counter and came over to shake our hands. "I'm Helena, Jade's mom. Where are you two lovely young ladies from?"

"Hi, I'm Sam. I go to school with Jade, I live down the road, and we are actually neighbors. And, um, this is my friend Kate, she lives in the city."

"Oh, Punxsutawney?" Helena asked Kate as she shook her hand.

"Oh no… I live in New York City. I'm just visiting for the weekend. But can I say, this had been the best thing I have seen so far! This house is friggin' amazing!" Kate said, staring at all the wonder that the kitchen had to hold.

"Oh, aha, the city. Well, if you girls would like, I am making my famous chili and corn bread for dinner, would you like to stay? We do dinner and a movie almost every Saturday night when the weather starts to turn! If it's after dark, I could drive you back home," Helena asked with eyes darting from us to her daughter in anticipation. Maybe she could sense that something was wrong with her daughter, and that she was pulling back from her friends.

I looked at Kate who was shaking her head up and down with approval.

"Well, I guess if that is okay with Jade, and I call my aunt and let her know." I looked at Jade, who was giving her mother a look that says, "Don't get into my business," but when she turned to me and genuinely smiled, I knew that it was okay.

Aunt Mimi was thrilled that we were inside the log house. She had been in it a couple of times and was raving about it on the phone.

"Tell your aunt that I am going to have to have her over soon!" Helena said while she was putting away groceries.

Jade, Kate, and I helped unload the groceries. Jade's father was away for the weekend with his hunting buddies, and Jade's younger sister Kylie was at a friend's for the night. So it was just us girls and Jade's mother.

"Do you want to sit on the porch? We can heat up some apple cider and chat," Jade asked while getting mugs out of the cabinet.

"Sounds perfect!" Kate said with a smile from ear to ear.

Helena was on a mission getting everything prepared for dinner, while we made ourselves comfortable on the giant porch. The air was crisp but not too cold. The sky was starting to turn from day into night, and I couldn't think of a better place to be enjoying this moment. The cider was delicious, and I felt like a small child in the giant rocking chair.

"Ahhhh, this is like the perfect place to come and just relax! Wow, I would die to live in a place like this!" Kate said as she laid completely back into an Adirondack-styled chair. She closed her eyes, and it would not surprise me one bit if she fell asleep.

Jade was fidgeting with her cup, rocking in the chair, not saying a word. I wanted to re-ask the question I asked before her mom came home, but I wasn't sure how to approach it.

"What you asked me earlier, I, um, well, I'm going through some things, and I…well, I just am having a hard time right now," Jade said while still fidgeting with her mug.

"Oh, I see… Have you talked to Mariah about it? I know she has been worried."

"Mariah wouldn't understand…neither would Rachel. I just, well, honestly I feel more alone than I ever have in my whole life," Jade said as tears started to form in the corners of eyes.

"Yeah, but they are your friends and they miss you. You shouldn't have to go through things on your own," I said, pleading with a girl that I barely knew.

"I know, I miss them too, it's better this way, though," she said as she shook her head and looked out into the fields on the other side of the road opposite the house.

"I'm sure they will understand. They have welcomed me in, and they didn't even know who I was. Without their friendship, man, I would be lost right now."

I proceeded to tell Jade about my dad, my mom, my former life, the recent turn of events at school, the counselor's office. Then…my experience with God, dance, my aunt and uncle's generosity, and up to present day. I don't know what compelled me to tell her everything, but I did and she was engrossed in my story. It felt good to tell it.

"Wow, I had no idea why you moved here. I don't know what to say," Jade said, looking at me with compassion.

"Yeah, it hasn't been an easy road, but I know I'm gonna make it," I said with complete confidence.

Jade was looking down at her mug with a look of concentration on her face.

"I want to tell you something, but you have to promise not to tell anyone, not Mariah, not Rachel, not Pastor Gloire or Ms. Yvonne, not anyone. Can I trust you?" Jade asked while looking at me directly in the eyes.

Kate was now snoring, so I could genuinely promise her. Although I was nervous for what she was going to tell me. Could I promise a girl I didn't even really know that I would keep her secret?

"I give you my word." Before I had a chance to contemplate, I spat out those words.

"Do you remember that boy Peter? The one who broke up with me a while back?" Jade asked without looking at me.

"Yeah, I remember, I think it was my first day of school," I said, knowing it was. I remembered fully... was happy the attention was off of me that day.

"Well, Peter and I dated for over a year. He didn't know God when we started dating, but he eventually started coming to church. It was great. I was in love for the first time, and well, he made a commitment to God, and everything was perfect," Jade said, and the tears started to form in the corners of her eyes again. "But little by little, things started to change. He would get upset easily, he was getting possessive, not wanting to hang out with friends and stuff. And well, I started allowing things to happen that I normally wouldn't let happen. And...one night, my parents went out, and Kylie was at a friend's house. Peter came over and we started messing around. Before I knew what was happening, we...well, ya know...it happened," Jade said as her face flushed a crimson red.

I could tell this was hard for her to say. What she didn't know is I was so used to hearing all kinds of things. *I mean, I am from one of the most liberal states in the country.*

"Oh, I see, well, Jade, we all make mistakes. I mean I have made plenty! It still doesn't make sense to me that you would leave all your friends for that."

"That's not all. I...well, Sam...I'm pregnant!" Jade said and put her head completely in her lap and started sobbing.

I immediately got up and went over to her and hugged her. I didn't know what else to do. My head was swirling. Now I know why she stopped dancing...but why did she stop everything else?

"I don't know what to do! I told Peter, and he wanted me to get an abortion! I said no way! He said he needed time to think, and just like that...he was with someone else. I can't go to church or hang out with my friends! I'm no good! My parents are going to kill me...I haven't told anyone except Ms. Rose at school, and now you," Jade said in between sobs.

"Jade, I'm so sorry about Peter...but I know that your friends are not the kind of friends that turn their backs on people. If the church doesn't accept you, then it should accept no one! And you are good! Just because you had a lapse in judgment doesn't mean that you aren't any good! None of us are any good then! We all sin, just like it says in the Bible. But you know we have a God that forgives us. Right?" I was questioning myself at this point, didn't this girl know more than me?

"You don't understand... I've been going to this church my whole life. It would be such an embarrassment to my family. At least if I leave now, when I have the baby, *if* I keep the baby, then I will have already separated myself from the church, and then it won't be so hard on my family."

Jade let out a large sigh as if relieved to have spilled her guts.

"I understand that you are thinking of your family, but honestly, what is best for you right now and your baby? May I ask how far along you are?" The question just shot out of my mouth, I didn't know what I could do, but this girl was in some serious trouble if she thought she could hide if from her family for much longer.

"The doctor at the clinic said that I am about nine weeks pregnant. I know I am going to start showing soon, and I don't know what to do." Jade said with such sadness.

"Well, I am not going to tell you what to do, but I do know that people that are around you love you, and if they really love you, then they will support you, Jade," I said with confidence.

"How do you know? How do you know that my family won't kick me out? How do you know that Mariah and Rachel won't look down on me?"

"I can't predict how people are going to react, but if it's any conciliation, you have my support. I know we don't know each other very well, but I am right down the road, and I am here whenever you want to talk. If you want to tell your friends or family, I can be here with you to, if you want." *I can't believe I'm offering this girl, who is really an acquaintance, my help. She probably is thinking I am nuts.*

"Sam, thank you so much. It feels so good to be able to tell someone. Thank you for not judging me or looking at me like I'm some kind of horrible person," Jade said and managed a small smile.

Jade's mother came barreling out of the door. "Ladies, dinner is ready!" she said with way too much enthusiasm.

"What? Where am I? Who?" Kate said as she jumped to her feet. Jade and I had a good laugh as reality came back to Kate.

The chili was amazing, but it was extremely spicy! I must have downed three glasses of water during consumption. After dinner, we watched *The Fault in Our Stars*, and we all cried throughout the whole thing. Kind of depressing for a Saturday evening, but the movie was really good and intense! After the movie, Helena took Kate and me home. Just as I thought, Jake and Brad were in the living room playing video games with an empty pizza box, chip bags, and six empty cans of soda. My predictions were correct.

Kate and I stayed up late again talking about college and where we would end up. With the lights off and Kate there with me, it felt like I was home in the city on a normal weekend, talking about the same things we would always talk about. I could almost feel my dad outside my room, watching TV sipping on coffee and eating popcorn. If only...

....

The morning was a little crazy as we had two more people to get ready for church. I was nervous about what Kate's reaction would be like; she was used to Catholic services, which are a little more reserved than the Assemblies of God. Sometimes Kate had no filter, so I was hoping she wouldn't embarrass the heck out of me!

Kate was just as amazed as I was the first time I saw the youth room. Kate and Gloire hit it off; she had him doubled over in laughter with her quick wit. I was able to breathe a little better after that. During worship, Kate was looking around a lot, observing. She was moving to the beat a bit and smiling. I could hear every once in a while a soft harmony coming out of her mouth. She was a singer and couldn't resist. After worship, I looked behind me to see what time it was and spotted a familiar face in the back. Jade caught my eye and smiled. I was so happy to see her there! Mariah and Rachel were sitting next to her and Mariah had her arms around Jade as if she wasn't going to let her go.

After church, we headed to Punxy Phil's Cakes and Steaks for a family dinner before Uncle Lou took Kate and Brad back to the city. We took Aunt Mimi's car and Uncle Lou's truck so we could all fit. Aunt Mimi didn't think it was a good idea for us to ride to the city and back because of school in the morning. I wasn't going to argue, I didn't like long car rides, and we had an amazing weekend. It was hard saying good-bye to Kate. We both had tears in our eyes, and Kate usually did not show emotion.

I headed to bed early. I was exhausted from a range of emotions. The excitement from having my best friend here, a night out on the town, the revelation from Jade, our late-night chats, everything we packed in a weekend was enough to fill an entire week. Even though I was beat, it didn't stop me from reading. I found myself reading almost every night. I never was much of a reader, but now, I wanted to learn more about my faith. I was intrigued by these stories in the Bible that just popped into life. I went to bed every night with my head filled with these amazing stories—and they're all true! My favorite so far is of a young woman who prepared for a year to go before the king! I can barely give myself an extra ten minutes to put makeup on in the morning! Talk about a strong woman, Esther, you got it hands down.

8

The Revelation

Monday came way too early. I breezed through my classes and was so happy it was lunchtime and half the day was finally over.

"Hey, Sam, how are you?" Jade asked as she sat down next to me at the lunch table. I was let out of class a couple minutes early to use the bathroom and thought I would be alone at the table for a few minutes.

"Hi, Jade! Are you going to sit here with us?" I said.

"Yeah, I thought a lot about what you said. I don't need to give up my friends. It's not going to be easy to tell them, but they mean a lot to me. I think I'm going to tell Mariah today."

"I'm so glad. I know she can handle it. Let me know if there is anything that you want me to do," I said, looking at her with understanding.

"Thanks, I actually would like you to be there, if you don't mind. Ms. Rose said I could have everyone come to her office, I'm not sure if I'm gonna do that or not."

"Well, whatever you decide, I'm there." Just as our conversation ended, Mariah and Rachel entered the lunchroom. But there was no Pat or Sam.

"Jade! Yay, your back with us at lunch too! I'm so glad! We missed your face," Mariah said as she grabbed Jade around the neck, forcing Jade to drop her apple.

"Well, thanks for the greeting, Riah, you almost knocked me over!" Jade said with a large smile.

"Yeah, well, ya'll know me, and you're more than likely going to drop a lot of things when I go in for a hug. What is up with you eating an apple anyway? What about the 'I'm eating anything I want until I'm old and can't handle it' motto? I never understood how a dancer ate such horrible things and maintained such a great figure! Anyways, what's with the change of heart? Have you finally listened to me? Oh my and yogurt too? Where is Jade, and what have you done with her?!"

Clearly Mariah had no clue that Jade was now eating for two people. Jade gave me a "please help me" look. She didn't answer Mariah and just continued to eat her healthy lunch.

Rachel grabbed Jade's hand from across the table and said, "Oh my gosh, Jade, you haven't seen Sam dance! She did a performance with the dance crew a few Sundays ago, and she is good! I bet Ms. Yvonne is going to be thrilled to have the both of you dancing together!"

Jade's face flushed a bit of red, and she looked in my direction. I didn't know what she was thinking. Was she upset that I was dancing with her crew? Was she embarrassed that she was no longer there? I didn't know her well enough to read her face.

"Well, I have some things going on right now, so I am not sure that I will return to dancing this year," Jade said as she looked down toward her pink lunch cooler that had a ballerina dancing in a white leotard on the front of it.

"Things going on? What *things*? You never used to miss a dance class or an opportunity to dance no matter what? What's going on? Can we help?" Mariah fired the questions away.

"Ugh, I can't take it anymore. Listen, I have something to tell the both of you and you cannot tell anyone and you cannot look at me differently, can you promise me that?" Jade asked with a firmness I hadn't seen from her yet.

"Yeah, most def," Rachel said.

"Yeah, of course, you know you can tell me anything," Mariah said with a concerned look.

I shook my head in agreement. I couldn't believe she was going to let it all out here in the lunchroom! What if the boys walked in? What if one of the kids in here overheard her? I was kinda happy that she was going to tell them this way, because now it won't look like I knew before Mariah and Rachel.

Jade proceeded to tell both of them all the gory details of her end of the relationship with Peter, her compromise, and his child whom she was now carrying. She didn't leave one detail out; she talked about why she pulled away, the church, and it was obvious why she stopped dancing.

"Wow," Rachel said while staring at Jade.

"I really don't know what to say," Mariah said with a sad expression on her face.

"That, that's what I'm talking about. You can't look at me like that!" Jade said, pointing toward Mariah's face.

"Look at you like what? I'm sorry this is a lot to take in, Jade, I'm concerned for you." Mariah said with all sincerity.

Just like that, the bell rang, and we all had to get back to class.

"Remember you promised not to say a word to anyone!" Jade said again with a very stern look.

"Yeah, we got it, of course!" Rachel said, shaking her head up and down, still with a look of shock on her face.

"Jade, I am here for you, and I want to talk more about this, please call me later," Mariah said as she gathered her book bag and gave Jade an extra long hug good-bye and took off with Rachel to catch their next class on the third floor.

"I wasn't expecting to tell them like that," Jade said with a look of disbelief on her face while shaking her head back and forth and running her fingers through her dark shiny hair.

"I'm not gonna lie, I was a little shocked myself. I think they handled it very well though." *I do think they handled it well; however, Rachel looks like she has seen a ghost!* Mariah was solid as usual.

Jade and I walked together until we parted ways for class. She said she was relieved that she was able to tell her friends, but she still had so many decisions to make, and she wasn't sure she was ready to be a mom. Boy was I glad I was not in the same predicament. I would royally screw up a kid if I had one right now. Sixteen-year-olds are not meant to be mothers, not in this day and age! But if you do get pregnant, what is the right thing to do? Man, I was feeling some type a way for Jade.

"And the answer to that question is what, Ms. Coal?" *I guess drifting off in English is not the best way to impress your teachers.* Mr. B. was staring at me with his hand on his hip with a smug smirk on his face.

"Um, sorry, could you repeat the question?" I asked, embarrassed that I was caught off guard. I looked around and felt a twinge better; everyone looked comatose at this point in the day.

"How does the underlying theme in Macbeth compare to other Shakespearian tragedies?"

Shakespeare! What the heck were we talking about! *Thank God we had to act his plays out at SOTA.*

"I think the underlying theme in most of his work revolves around human ambition and greed, and what lengths people will go to get what they want. Often in his work resulting in betrayal, murder, great deceit, and ultimately regret." I had no idea where that came from, but thank Jesus he was with me today! I actually sounded like I knew what I was talking about!

Mr. B. just stared at me for a moment then proceeded. "Okay, thank you, Sam. Does anyone agree or disagree with Sam? Does anyone have anything that they would like to add before we move on?"

The statement opened up discussion and the rest of the time went by pretty quickly. When the bell rang, I was more than thrilled to go.

"Good job today, Sam, I hope you will continue to give your input," Mr. B. said as he nodded.

I nodded back, that was the first time he had spoken to me. I was averaging a B+ in his class, not too bad. Everyone talks about how hard he is and how much work he gives out. I felt like a literary genius as I made my way through the rest of the day.

When I got home, Aunt Millie was busy getting supper ready early because of my dance schedule. I had to be there at 5:00 p.m. today to meet with Ms. Yvonne for my first one-on-one dance lesson with her. I didn't want to be late. I still could not believe that she was giving out free lessons! She would be getting so much money for lessons in the city. I had never known such selfless people in all my life—well, besides my dad and my aunt and uncle, but they were family.

Ms. Yvonne was waiting in the youth room when I arrived. She was stretching to a slow song that I didn't recognize.

"Well, hello, Sam!" Ms. Yvonne came over and gave me a big hug.

"Hi, sorry, I'm a few minutes late. Unfortunately, we had to wait for a train to pass," I said, feeling terrible, even though it was only 5:03 p.m. when I walked in.

"Ha, it is not late, no worries, let's stretch out a bit then we can get started!" Ms. Yvonne had a twinkle in her eyes when she smiled. I could tell I was going to love coming here for lessons.

Ms. Yvonne had me show her all the jumps that I knew as well as any combinations that I had perfected over the years. She pushed me to my limit, seeing what I was able to do. The time went by so fast I didn't even see the students gathering in the room.

"Sam, you have amazing lines, you're graceful, and I can tell you have a passion for dance. I can't wait to work on a piece with you for competition!" Ms. Yvonne said as she shifted her concentration to the students who had arrived for our regular Monday practice.

With the crew, we practiced a new routine that had some complex parts. Three other dancers and I in the Queens group had mini solos. It was to be performed for their Christmas program that they do every year. I guess it was a pretty big deal for the people in Big Run. The dance crew kept talking about how the church was packed to the max last year and people had to stand in the back. When practice was over, I was actually quite happy about it. I was sore from lack of practice mixed with being pushed from Ms. Yvonne to see my abilities as a dancer. I was sore, but a happy sore.

Tuesday came and went. I went over to Jade's after school and spent the afternoon working on homework and had dinner with her and her family. She was still not sure when or how she was going to tell her parents. Jade was a thin girl, not too skinny, but thin enough that her baby bump was going to show very soon. As a matter of fact, if you looked closely, you could see the slightest bump. I kept encouraging her to tell her parents; her mom seemed nice enough and her dad, while reserved, doted on his family. She needed to see more than the school nurse! She didn't want to go to her doctor because it would show up on the insurance bills that went directly to her parents. I guess I could understand that, but all the more reason to be honest with them. I again told her that I would be there when she told them if she wanted to, Mariah had offered the same thing.

By lunchtime on Wednesday, I was so completely exhausted I didn't know what to do with myself. It was only hump day! I plopped down at our usual lunch table and waited for everyone. Out of the corner of my eye, I noticed a familiar face coming toward me. This girl was dressed in black from head to toe, dyed black hair, nails painted black, and big scowl on her face. It all of a sudden dawned on me; she was one of the girls that Jade had been sitting with while she was on hiatus from the group. She was also the girl at the bus stop that scowled at me the first day I was here.

"Hey, can you give this to Jade." The angry-looking girl handed me a folded-up piece of paper.

"Uh, sure, no problem." With that, she turned and walked away, leaving no explanation.

Pat and Sam came first, then Mariah, Rachel, and Jade. They all bought lunch today; it was pizza, and I guess I didn't get the memo.

"Oh, Sam, this is the best pizza! Why didn't you buy today? The school only gets real pizza a few times a year?" Mariah said while placing the amazing-looking giant slice of pie next to me.

"I had no idea that was even an option. Had I known, I may have indulged! That looks good!" I said while my mouth lay watering, dreading the yogurt and fruit I had awaiting consumption.

"Jade, really? You're gonna eat as much as Pat and me?" Sam said, looking at her lunch tray like it was some kind of foreign object; Jade had bought an extra slice like the boys.

"Leave her alone! She's hungry!" Rachel said while frowning at Sam and Pat who were laughing now. Rachel was trying to be protective of Jade, but all she did was draw more attention. At this point, Jade's face had turned beet-red.

"Hey, Jade, some girl came over here and asked me to give this to you," I said, hoping to change the subject while handing her the folded-up piece of paper. Jade looked perplexed while she opened the paper. Everyone was watching. I, all of a sudden, wished that I had waited until we were alone to give it to her.

Jade's face turned from red to white. She quickly folded it back up and looked down at her lunch tray. She started eating slowly.

"Well? What was the note about, Jade? Are you really not going to tell us anything?" Pat said annoyingly, like it was his business to know everyone else's.

"Really, Pat?" Rachel said as she threw a dirty napkin in his direction.

"Wow, Rachel, when did you girls get so temperamental? Geez," Pat said and took an enormous bite of his pizza. Sam and Mariah were watching the exchange in amusement. I was focused on Jade who was looking a little green at this point. She got up from the table, grabbed her things, and ran out of the lunchroom; everyone froze.

"She looked like she might be sick," Sam said compassionately.

"I'll go check on her. I'll catch up with you guys later," I said while packing up my stuff. The rest of the group said good-bye while Mariah gave me a *knowing* look. I headed out of the cafeteria and went straight to the bathroom I had my *own* meltdown in front of.

I could hear her sniffling in one of the stalls.

"Jade, it's me. Do you want to talk about it? No one else is in here right now." The toilet flushed and slowly Jade came out of the stall and washed her hands in the sink. She looked at me with a tear-stained face.

"That was Peter's sister, Camille, who gave you the letter. She was dressed all in black, right?" Jade said with a questioning face.

"Yeah, it was one of the girls I saw you sitting with earlier this month," I said, hoping I was going to be able to help this girl somehow. Wow. Peter and his sister were way different from one another. Peter was an athlete, he was actually a really good football player for the school, and his sister looked like an extra on American Horror Story!

Jade handed me the now crumpled-up letter for me to read. Who gives letters now anyway? Does he not know how to text?

> Jade, I'm sorry that you think that this is my kid, but do you have any proof? Do not tell anyone about this, or I will not make going to school here very easy for you. I have a possible full ride scholarship out of this pathetic town, and I'm not going to let some possible mistake keep me here, all because you wouldn't go on birth control, or end the pregnancy. I hope you get this message clearly.
>
> Peter

"Jade...I don't even know what to say. I'm so angered right now." *I want to run screaming out of this bathroom, find Peter, and kick him where it would really hurt. But I have to stay calm for Jade.*

"I...I...can't...believe...he...is treating me...this way," Jade said in between sobs. I had no way to console her. I had no words of comfort. That's when I realized I could pray.

"Jade, can I pray for you?" I asked. She nodded in agreement. "God, I know that you can hear me, right? I know you see this situation. I ask that you would give Jade peace right now where we are standing. God, we ask for your grace and mercy. God, I also ask that you give Jade the perfect timing to tell her parents, and we ask that you would be in the middle of that conversation. God, can you please let Peter know how hurtful that he is being? Also can you help me not want to punch him in the face right now, because there is not much holding me back. In Jesus's name, AMEN!"

Jade opened her eyes looked at me and started to giggle. We both started to laugh. It seemed that God answered my prayer immediately.

"Oh my goodness, Sam, you are too much! Hahahaaa. I can't remember the last time I laughed like that!" Jade said through a tear-stained smile.

"Well, I was being honest. Me and the big guy are getting to know each other, and I know that I can totally be honest with how I'm feeling with God. And right then and there, I wanted nothing more than to punch Peter in the face and kick him where it would really hurt...so I figured I should pray about that too!"

Jade kept laughing and looked in the mirror and started to clean her face. She turned sideways, and you could see a tiny little curve on her once-flat stomach. She breathed in and sighed heavily.

"Well, I guess today is as good as any to tell my parents. I can't hold off much longer anyway. What are you doing this afternoon? Want to be part of another giant revelation?" Jade asked with hopeful eyes.

"I said I would be there if you wanted me to, and I will. I have nothing after school, except Amped later on, and we can go together if you still plan on going," I said as I leaned in and gave her a hug. "It will be okay, you will get through this."

"Yeah, should be fun! Hey, Mom, Dad, I'm pregnant!" Jade said through a nervous chuckle. Just as she said it, the stall on the farthest left flushed and a girl from the cheerleading squad came out of the stall. Looked at me, then at Jade, washed her hands, and left without saying a word.

"Jade, I'm so sorry! I didn't see anyone or hear anyone in here!" I said, and I could feel my face flush.

"Oh my gosh, that was Tara Jones. She is on the varsity cheer squad. She cheers for Peter's team!" Jade held her stomach and leaned forward.

"Are you okay? What's the matter? Are you going to be sick?" I asked in a panicked voice.

"I'm fine, I didn't hear anyone else in here either, and she was probably doing something she shouldn't that's why she was so quiet. I hope she doesn't tell anyone or approach Peter. I think I'm going to be sick," and with that, Jade ran to the stall and the little bit of lunch she actually did eat came up and out.

I walked Jade to the nurse's office and got a late pass to my English class. I was really hoping that Jade would be okay; I was nervous about having to be there when she told her parents. I mean, I didn't really know them all that well. I was just getting to know them. I told her I would support her, so that I would do.

9

Ghosts of Christmas Past

Uncle Joe picked us up at the bus stop, and he was even more quiet than usual; he didn't even look in our direction. He just sighed a few times. I was hoping that we didn't do anything to upset him, or maybe he was just sick of having to pick up two kids every day from the bus stop. When I got home, I planned on changing and walking to Jade's house. It was odd; there was an old Buick Lacrosse in the driveway. I didn't recognize the car; maybe Aunt Mimi had one of her friends over from the women's ministry at the church. Or maybe she was being tortured by some Mary Kay consultant—who knew. I hurried up the stairs of the porch, beating Jake. I wanted to be at Jade's as soon as I could; I wasn't sure when she was going to tell her parents, and I wanted to make sure I was there to help calm her nerves.

I opened the door, and I was hit in the face with a familiar smell. It was Chanel No. 5. I knew that perfume all too well. In front of me was the backside of a woman with brown hair that shined all the way to the middle of her back. Aunt Mimi was sitting across from her and had a nervous grin on her face and was playing with her hands. The woman stood up and turned and faced me while smoothing out the pleats in her beige dress pants. My heart stopped, and I had to gasp for air. I was shouting in my head, but no words came to the surface. The long legs, shiny flowing hair, those piercing eyes, and new crow's feet that had formed in the corners of her eyes. It had been over eight years since I had last seen her.

"Mom! Mom, is that really you?" Jake pushed past me and stood before the woman who was now a stranger to us.

"Yes, yes, Jake, it's me," my *mother* said through a tear-stained face. She grabbed Jake and hugged him with all her might. Jake just let it happen. I stood there like a deer in headlights as she put out her hand for me to come join in for some kind of group hug. I just stood there staring at her. I couldn't move. Aunt Mimi came over to me and put her arm around me.

"Sam and Jake, your mother came here today because she wanted to see you. I had no idea she was coming. This is a surprise for all of us," Aunt Mimi said while hugging me from the side tightly.

"I know that I have a lot of explaining to do, I just couldn't wait any longer to see you. I just heard about your father and I am so sorry," the stranger said.

The minute she mentioned my father, I could feel my blood boiling to the point of bursting. I picked up my book bag, which I had not even noticed that I had dropped, and ran into my bedroom and slammed the door. It was seconds before my face flooded with tears.

How could she just show up here! Who does she think she is! How can she even mention my dad! Did I really just see my mother? How could Jake even hug that woman! How could my aunt let her in the house! My mind was racing, and I was so full of anger I was afraid of what I would do if anyone came into my room. I laid on the bed, and out came Niagara Falls until I heard a knock on my door.

"Sam, you have a phone call," my aunt said in a concerned tone.

Shoot! I forgot about Jade!

"Okay, hold on." I wiped the tears from my face and opened the door. My aunt handed me the phone, and she put her hand on my shoulder. She had tears of compassion in her eyes. I didn't care; I was in the land of confusion, hurt, and anger and I didn't know how to respond to anything at the present time. I took the phone and closed the door behind me.

"Hello, Jade?" I tried to sound as normal as humanly possible. "I'm so sorry. I had a situation here at home, and I can be over in a few minutes," I said, hoping that she would be understanding.

"No worries, thanks for the offer. I just called to let you know that I left school early, my mom picked me up. I was so upset, I actually told her on the way home," Jade said with a calm demeanor. I was hoping that this meant things went well.

"Oh, wow, how did it go?" I asked

"Not as bad as I thought. My mom cried and then hugged me. She is sad more than angry. She said she didn't see the point in grounding me seeing that I had enough punishment all on my own, with Peter and all. We plan on telling my father after dinner tonight. Please say a prayer for me! By the way, what happened over there?" I could feel my breaths getting shorter. I was trying to focus on the conversation, but my head was spinning in fifty different directions.

"I'm so glad to hear that Jade, I will pray for you tonight. Let me know how it goes," I said, avoiding the last question.

"Okay, I will, and thanks again for being there for me. You have no idea how amazing your friendship has been."

"Hey, no problem, and I'm glad to be there. I'm just a phone call away if you need to talk," I said and I meant it. Jade and I were getting closer, and I could tell we were going to be good friends. And I was definitely going to need all the support I could get. I waited a few minutes before I returned the phone to the kitchen where that woman and my aunt were. I had no idea how Jake was feeling, I wanted to punch something. When I got out into the kitchen, the only one there was my aunt. I placed the phone back on the charger and was about to walk back into my bedroom.

"Sam, are you okay?" my aunt asked with hesitation.

"Yeah, I'm fine," I said matter-of-factly, but really, I think I was in shock.

"Will you sit with me for a minute?" she asked as she settled down at the kitchen table and patted the place mat on the opposite side of the table. I sat down, staring down at the place mat. I never noticed the saying on the placemat until now. *Count your age by friends, not years; count your life by smiles, not tears.* Nice quote. Now I can skip and join hands with everyone and sing kumbaya—fat chance.

"Sam, I am so sorry how this just happened. I know your emotions must be on overload." Aunt Mimi patted my hand from across the table.

"Where is she?" I asked, not really wanting to know, on the same hand desperately wanting to know.

"She and your brother went out." My aunt had an apologetic look on her face. "Grace, I mean, your mom, wanted you to go with them, but she wasn't sure you wanted to talk right now."

That was an understatement. My heart sank with betrayal, how could my brother just leave with her? I didn't want to talk, that was for sure. I wanted to scream at that woman until her ears popped! And what the heck, Jake!? Is he out skipping through town with that woman? She had no clue how much she tore our family to pieces. I can remember my dad walking around the house like he was a zombie. Jake and I having to make ourselves dinner, pack our own lunches, and get ourselves ready for school, and we were in elementary school! My father lost his job because of how much time he missed. We lost our house and had to go on food stamps. We moved into a run-down, one-bedroom apartment in the worst part of the hood. How can I even look at a woman that caused the people I hold nearest and dearest to my heart so much pain?

One day, something finally snapped, and my father woke up out of his oblivion. He found a good job and we worked ourselves back into a decent apartment in the city, that wasn't rat- and bug-infested. I was able to attend dance class again and attend the School of the

Arts. It took our family so much time to heal. Now my dad is gone, and she thinks she can just swoop in here and save the freakin' day? I think not.

"Yeah, I definitely don't want to talk to her right now. I just don't get how she can just pop in here like she was gone to the grocery store for eight years and now she's back," I said, not looking my aunt in the eyes.

My aunt sighed. I could tell she was searching for just the right words to say, to make me feel sorry for that woman, or make me forgive; well, *nothing* she could say could make me change my mind—nothing. As far as I knew, that woman was the enemy. I have had enemies before and none of them could have possibly made me feel like than woman.

"Sam, I can definitely understand how you are feeling. This is a shock to all of us." I had never seen my aunt look so sad. I wondered how this was making her feel. She hadn't seen her sister in so many years, had no idea where she was, and now had two of her sister's brats to feed. Would she make us go with that woman? I was starting to feel sick inside; just when I thought I could get used to the new normal, a monkey wrench was thrown in the mix. How could I ever go anywhere with *her*?

"Aunt Mimi, are we going to have to go with her?" I blurted out without much thought behind it.

Aunt Mimi looked at me with a look of confusion, then a small smile formed in the corner of her mouth.

"Sam, you have no idea how much joy you and your brother have brought into this home. This is your home for as long as you want to live here. I have no idea what your mother's plans are at this time. Of course, if she decides to stay here to be close to you and Jake, you can change your mind anytime you want. But please understand that you will always have a home here."

I felt a warm rush of relief flow through my body. I got up from the table, ran over to my aunt, fell down next to her chair, and hugged my aunt as hard as I could. And then it started. I have never cried so much in my life as I have in these past couple of months. My aunt just held me as I buried my face, nestled into her side, and she held me tight. I have no idea how long I was sitting there, but when I was emptied out, I got up and got some tissues. My aunt was wiping tears from her own eyes. I brought the box of Kleenex to her and sat back down across the table from her. We just sat in silence for a while, then the inevitable happened.

The door opened and there stood Jake, that woman, and my uncle. Did Uncle Lou go with them? The woman looked at me with pathetic eyes. Jake didn't make eye contact with me, said good-bye to the woman, and went into his room. I couldn't look at her directly; I thought my eyes might burn and roll into the back of my head like I was staring at some sort of a demon from a horror flick. My uncle put his hat away and went and sat in his chair, propped his feet up, and started rummaging through the paper.

"Samantha, can I sit down?" the woman asked me as if I had any control over where she sat her butt down.

"It's a free country," I said without looking anywhere but down at that god-awful placemat.

The woman named Grace sat ever so carefully in the empty chair in between me and my aunt. She acted as if she thought the chair was going to break.

"Samantha, I am sorry for just showing up like this out of the blue. I didn't take into consideration how difficult it might be for you to see me. I would like the opportunity to explain myself if you would allow me to do that," the woman said while she was nervously playing with her hands.

I didn't know what to say. I was definitely curious about where she had been for half my life; maybe a phone call every couple of years would have been nice! Or how about a surprise visit on mine or Jake's birthday when we were so young, sitting there on those sacred days; just knowing she was not going to be able to stay away from her children that she said she *loved* so much on their birthdays! No, I wasn't going to give her the satisfaction or the opportunity to explain herself; she had ample time to do so in the past. What makes now so special?

I was disgusted with the whole situation; I needed to leave. I could not take it any longer. I got up, grabbed my jacket from the coat rack by the door, and turned and faced her; my face was on fire. I looked her directly in her eyes.

"No, I don't want to know anything about you. I waited for years. I waited for you to come back to the kids you just 'adored' so much. I waited for you to come and rescue Dad from his depression. I waited for you to be there for me when I had questions Dad couldn't answer! I waited for you every night until my fourteenth birthday, then something finally clicked. You weren't my mother. Mothers don't abandon their children. Mothers love their families and would never give up on them. And a good wife would never leave her husband who adored her. My father was a mother and a father to me." My mouth started quivering, and I was about to lose it. "So I don't care what you have to say. You're not my mother and you don't owe me any explanations."

With that, I left them all standing there and took off out the door and started running down the road. I was having a hard time seeing through my salty tears. My nose was dripping like a four-year-old with a severe cold. Before I knew it, I was standing outside of Jade's house knocking on the door.

Jade's mother opened the door with a forlorn look on her face.

"Hi, Samantha, now's really not a good…honey, what happened? Are you okay?" Helena was looking at me like I had four heads. To her credit, I did have snot dripping down my face, probably bloodshot eyes, and I was panting like a thirsty animal.

"Yeah, I'm okay, is Jade home?" I asked, praying that she would let me inside.

Jade came to the door with a face that probably resembled mine; in all the craziness, I forgot what was happening today.

"Hey," Jade said with a sad look in her eyes. Jade's mother went back inside.

"Hey, I'm sorry to just show up like this," I said while wiping the snot from my face with my sleeve, trying not to think about it so I wouldn't gag.

"It's fine, come on in," she said, and I walked in and closed the door behind me.

From the foyer, I could see Jade's dad sitting on the couch in the living room from the side view. He had his head in his hands, not saying a word. Jade and I went up to her bedroom in the loft. She closed the door behind her ever so gingerly; I guess trying not to disturb the peace? I sat in her reading chair, and she sat on her bed facing in my direction. She looked awful.

"Jade, I'm so sorry to show up like this. It was careless thinking. I guess I wasn't thinking at all."

"Sam, it's really fine, I was gonna call you anyway. It didn't go as well with my dad as it did with my mom, as if you couldn't tell…" Jade said with one lonely tear sliding down her face.

"I'm sorry, Jade, do you want to talk about it?" I asked, feeling a little guilty for intruding on their family in the middle of this situation. Jade sighed for a moment then looked at me intently for a moment, pulling in her eyebrows. "Sam, have you been crying?"

I looked up at her, then down toward the thick, light-blue carpet. I loved the way my feet felt underneath her floor; it was like walking on pillows. "Yeah, I have been. I felt like a complete moron for showing up like this. I just wanted to get the heck out of my house, and this is where I ended up."

"What happened?" Jade asked, leaning in to get the scoop.

I really felt selfish at the moment. How could I just show up like this? What in the world was I thinking? Jade looked like she was emotionally drained, and here I was, about to unload my adolescent angst on her.

"Jade, you first, I can't apologize enough about my insensitivity to this emotional roller coaster you must be on right about now. What can I do to help?" I rested my hands neatly in my lap and put on my best listening face.

"Sam, seriously? You insensitive? Whenever you are with me, all you think about is how you can help. Honestly, I wouldn't mind taking my mind off my own problems for a minute. I really want to know what is going on," Jade said with a pleading gaze. I figured I would appease her.

"You know how I ended up here in Big Run already, so I won't bore you with those deets…but what you may not know is that my 'mother' abandoned Jake and me when I was about eight years old. Well, when I came home from school today, guess who decided to finally *grace* us with her presence."

Sarcasm always came naturally to me. *That* I got from my dad. I found it a comforting way to get out my feelings without having to be too vulnerable.

"Wow. I really don't even know what to say. Is she still there? What did you do?" Jade's eyes were wide with intrigue.

"Well, I didn't handle it like a happy child who found their lost parent. I can reassure you that much. Jake must feel differently than I do. He went out with her for a while, while I stayed back and saturated my pillow."

"Sam, that's tough. I have no idea how I would even begin to respond to that." Jade was shaking her head in disbelief.

"Yeah, I may or may not have said some of the mean thoughts that were ramming through my brain. I have a hard time holding in how I feel, sometimes to the detriment of everyone around me," I said, thinking about the awkward situation I left my aunt to deal with in the wake of my episode.

"It's completely understandable. How would anyone react in that kind of situation? We all handle grief in our own way. I will be here whenever you want to talk, pray, whatever you need, just give me call. Or you can always just run down the street to my door," Jade said with a smirk.

We both laughed.

"Now it's your turn…what happened today with your dad?" I asked.

Jade let out a sigh, returning to the undeniable issue that was starting to deform her firm teenage belly.

"Well, I can honestly say I am relieved that part is over with. It was hard watching my dad's initial reaction of shock and unbelief turn into an expression of pure disappointment. One thing I never thought I would attain, breaking my parents' hearts," Jade said as another lonely tear rolled down her face.

"He will get over it…eventually. He has to, right? Besides, your mom handled it well, and she will be a good voice in his ear," I said with confidence, although unsure about it. I didn't even know her parents well enough to make that statement.

"My dad says that there is no way that I am old enough to raise a baby, and if I choose to keep it, he doesn't want me living here. He said it's a bad influence on my sister," Jade said with a shaky voice, and then the tears started to fall.

I went over to her and put my arms around her. I started praying. I can't even remember what I was saying, all I know is I was hoping that God was hearing both of our cries. If He is truly all that we need, then He hears our cries and will answer, right? All I know is, I didn't know what else to do or what else to say. Jade came up for a breather and grabbed some tissues off her desk and handed some to me; we were both a blubbering mess.

"I honestly don't know what I'm gonna do. I don't know if adoption is the right choice for me. There are no other options for me other than raising it on my own. I don't know if I could give up my own child, and I don't know if I could raise a baby on my own! I can't believe I let my guard down, and I have to deal with this! I should be worrying about what I'm going to wear to the Christmas dance, my future in dancing and college, and who I want to go with to the prom! But no, I have to worry about prenatal vitamins, doctor's appointments, and the future of my child!" Jade said with an exasperated voice.

I just sat there listening while she poured out her soul. I had no words of advice. I could only listen and offer my support that way.

Knock, knock, knock. "Who is it?" Jade asked as if it could be a numerous amount of people.

"Jade, it's time for dinner. Sam, are you staying?" Helena asked.

Jade shook her head in approval with pleading eyes.

"Sure, if that's all right?" I asked.

"Yep, that's fine. I'll call your aunt and let her know." I could hear her footsteps grow farther and farther away.

"Thanks, I don't know if I could make it through the first meal without you here," Jade said, shaking her head back and forth.

"No problem, actually, I'm partially being selfish. I really don't want to go home right now." Jade gave me a reassuring hug, and we headed down the stairs.

I think Helena went out of her way to make a feast to overcompensate for the tension, but it didn't matter. Jade's father fixed himself a plate and then went into his den and shut the door. Jade's face turned three shades of red. I felt bad for the poor girl. Yeah, she made a mistake. Did they not understand how much she was going through right now? Did they forget how hard it was to be a teenager with all our raging hormones? Jade needed support, and maybe a little bit more conversation and talk about sex would have helped her make a different decision! I was fighting back my tongue because it wanted to unleash.

"What's up his butt?" Jade's little sister asked.

"Kylie Marie! We don't talk like that at the dinner table, and you do not refer to your father that way!" Helena spoke sternly, a little on the rough side from the norm, I could tell by the way Jade and Kylie reacted.

"Sheesh, you would think we have been invaded by aliens the way ya'll are acting!" Kylie said and then shoved her face with a mouthful of brown-sugared butternut squash.

The rest of the meal was quite uneventful. The silence was uncomfortable, but at least there were no outbursts.

Helena drove me home in silence until we reached the driveway. She stopped the car and then busted out crying. I had no idea what to say; I didn't know her very well, and quite frankly, she was supposed to be the adult! I just sat there, not saying a word until finally she stopped. I handed her a napkin I found on the seat behind me.

"Thank you, I'm sorry I just lost it. I have been holding that inside all day long. I want to be strong for the family, but I am so disappointed and heartbroken for my daughter. She has no idea what she is in for, believe me. Raising a teen when you are a teen is no picnic." Helena blew her nose, and I wanted to jump out of the car. What did she expect from me?

"I really don't know what to say except that Jade already feels ashamed and unsure of her future. You know, she almost turned her back on her friends and the church because of how she might be judged. What she needs the most right now is support and to know how much she is still loved." *I feel like a stinkin' therapist.*

"How did you get so smart, young lady?" Helena asked with a small grin.

"Believe me, I'm not. I have my moments." *Thinking about my own dilemma awaiting me inside the house.*

"Well, Jade is extremely lucky to have someone like you in her life. You are welcome at our house whenever. The door is always open." Helene gave me a hug and a kiss on the cheek. I guess that was my cue to leave. I was dreading the initial opening of the door to my aunt and uncle's house. Luckily, the woman's car was gone, and I didn't have to face her again—at least not for tonight.

"Good night, thanks for dinner. It was amazing, and your daughter is pretty awesome too. I'm just as lucky to have her in my life." Helena smiled and waved. She waited until I opened the door before pulling out of the driveway.

When I went inside, there was no movement; all the lights were off except for the porch and the hallway. Everyone must have went to bed early. I was happy to not have the confrontation tonight or any sort of talk on the subject. I was mentally drained and ready to pull the covers up and over my head for at least eight hours. I turned the porch light off and headed to my room. The air was chilly; there was an extra comforter folded neatly on the end of my bed. My aunt thought about what I needed before I knew I needed it. She would have been a great mom. I wonder why she never had any kids, or maybe my mom was so much to deal with when she was younger, she said forget it! I don't want any kids! The extra comforter was heaven. It was made of down, and I felt like I was being caressed by giant clouds. If only I could stop obsessing about the fact that my long-lost mother found her way back to her deserted and now fatherless kids. What made her come back? And why now? I couldn't stop asking myself the same questions over and over again. I must have stopped obsessing because it seemed like only minutes passed until my alarm was screaming at me.

I was going through the motions of the day, not really paying attention to anyone or anything. Sam was waving his hand in front of my face at study hall, wondering why my eyes were so glazed over. I didn't want to trouble him with more drama; he had enough to worry about all on his own. He and I were going for our usual coffee outing this Friday to talk about the woes of having lost a parent. If it comes up, then it comes up. We usually talked a bit then spent the rest of the time quoting funny movie lines and making each other laugh. He was fun to be around. Everyone was always asking if we were together. I say, "Yup, we were together last weekend, and we are going to be together next weekend!" I get annoyed, because apparently guys and girls can no longer have platonic relationships. Whatever. I wasn't going to worry about what other people were saying. It's funny when you go through something like Sam and I have; you no longer care about the petty gossip and idle talk that our lovely generation loves to plague themselves with. Sam was my friend, and I wasn't going to put a label on anything.

"Sam! Where in the heck were you last night? And you too, Jade?! It was an awesome service, oh my goodness, and, Sam, we really need to get you a phone." Mariah was looking between Jade and me like we had some sort of conspiracy going on and missed Amped because of it. I had completely forgotten in all the craziness that we missed youth group last night. It was the furthest thing from my mind, and I'm sure Jade's as well.

"Oh yeah, I forgot about youth group. Well, I had a very revealing discussion with my parents last night," Jade said, making her eyes wide for Mariah and Rachel to catch on while leaving Pat and Sam in the dark.

"Oh, okay, gotcha. We'll catch up later, and what about you, Ms. Thang! What kept you away?" Mariah asked me while tapping her fingers on the lunch table with a playful smirk on her face.

Out of the corner of my eye, I saw a bunch of cheerleaders approaching the table; one of them just happened to be the girl I saw Peter with the first day I met Jade. My heart started doing flip-flops, I made eye contact with Jade, and I could tell she was terrified. There were five of them, all wearing "love pink" jogging suits, and they stopped dead in front of Jade.

"Jade, would you mind coming with us? We have a few questions we would like answered." The tall blond one in the middle had her hands on her perfect hips, waiting for a reply from Jade. The girl from the bathroom was next to her, throwing out ridiculous-looking faces. If they were supposed to make us scared, they were working, but not in the way she wanted. So ridiculous.

"Um, not right now, I'm eating lunch," Jade said matter-of-factly.

"Okay, so if you want me to ask you in front of your little lunch table, then so be it," the tall blonde asked with a sinister smile.

Jade gathered her things in a flash, threw me a look of desperation, and followed the girls over to their table. I followed right behind her. If she needed me to kick some blemish free, bleach-blond cheer freak butt, I would be the girl for the job. With pleasure.

The girls sat down, offered for Jade to sit, and ignored me completely. I sat anyway.

"Well, we have heard some news, and I just want to confirm. I heard from a little birdie that you have a bun in the oven, and it may just be in fact from *my* current boyfriend. I need to know if these allegations have any truth to them," the girl asked with a calm, demanding demeanor. I could feel the chill in the air and was horrified for my friend. How quickly news travels, and she was in no shape to be having to handle all this added stress to an already stressful situation. I had no idea what she was going to say; her face was as red as a radish.

"I'm not really sure who told you this, but I am pretty sure that my relationship status is none of your concern. I'm also pretty sure that you are with Peter now, and if you have any questions about our past, you can get the information that you desire from him." Jade looked calm as a cucumber on the outside, but I knew better. She was ready to scream on the inside.

The girl gave a sharp annoyed look to the girl that I'm pretty sure was the little birdie and replied with a vengeance, "I knew Peter was telling the truth. Besides, he said you were a mistake that was completely forgotten when he knew I was interested in him. You and your pathetic little friend can leave now." The girl got up and leaned forward. "But if I find out that you are holding out on me, you can bet that pretty little head of yours that I will make life very hard for you, do you understand me?" She sat back down and folded her hands on the table with a smug look on her face. Her friends all had the same look and were waiting for us to leave.

Jade didn't go back to our table; she gathered her stuff and headed out of the cafeteria. I followed her out, looking back at a questioning Mariah. I felt bad; I knew that Mariah and Jade were close, but our friendship just sort of happened. I know that Jade values her friendship like no other and would fill her in on what was happening as soon as she was able to catch her breath!

"What just happened? Oh my gosh. I don't even know what to do! Pretty soon, the whole school is going to know, and Peter will deny that it's his—he already said so! They are going to think I just randomly slept with someone, and now I'm pregnant? Oh my gosh, Sam, please tell me, what should I do? Should I quit school? It looks like I might have to," Jade said with exasperation and seemed to be having a hard time breathing.

"Okay, right now, I just need you to calm down and breathe." I took Jade's book bag and led her to the drinking fountain.

"We don't know that those girls are going to say anything. If she is dating Peter, then she will probably not want that information blasted through the school anyway." Jade's breathing started to even out. I had no idea what she was going to do; she was already showing a tiny bit, but sooner rather than later, she was going to really show, and it was going to be undeniable that she was pregnant. For now, she needed more time to process this whole thing and make some decisions.

"Do you want to go talk to Ms. Rose? I'll go with you if you want," I asked, not knowing what else to do.

"Yeah, if you wouldn't mind, I would like you to be there. You seem to be more levelheaded than anyone else in my life right now." Jade took back her book bag, and we headed to the counselor's office.

Ms. Rose was in with a student, so we had to wait in the main office until she was free. The secretary gave us passes to get back to class when we were done. Jade was staring off when Ms. Rose came to get us. I had to call her name twice before she responded. Poor girl. I could not imagine being in her shoes. It was heart breaking to watch my friend suffer the consequence of one night of sex.

10

Forgive and Forget, Forget It

Ms. Rose was able to convince Jade's parents to meet with her and Jade together. The appointment was set for next Wednesday. Jade only had five days to avoid conversation with her father before the set date. Ms. Rose opened up to us while we were in the office. She told Jade that she was an adoptee. She was able to share with Jade about her feelings toward adoption versus keeping the baby. I'm not sure she was supposed to give her opinions like that, but geez, she held nothing back! I think Jade left even more confused. Ms. Rose was adopted into a decent family, but she never felt like she belonged. She thought it was best for the baby, for the whole family to come together to help Jade. You could see the passion in Ms. Rose's face; she must have really gone through it…but what was the best decision for Jade? Only she knew; no one else could make that decision for her. I was just praying that her family would support her no matter what decision she made.

The weekend didn't come soon enough; so much had taken place this week, and I was ready for a relaxing couple of days, I didn't even feel like going out with my friends. When I walked in the door, my aunt was running around as busy as ever cooking.

"Hello, Sam and Jake, how was your day?" my aunt asked while she was washing veggies in the sink.

"Eh, nothing new," Jake said with his mouth full of an apple that he took from the giraffe-painted fruit bowl on the table.

"Well, drama, drama, and more drama at school, Aunt Mimi. I am so ready for sleeping in, sipping on hot cocoa, and watching movies all weekend!" I said as I slouched into the kitchen chair.

Aunt Mimi slowly turned around while wiping her hands on the kitchen towel that had roosters on it.

"Um, well, I didn't have time to ask you two, but your mother is coming here for dinner tonight." Aunt Mimi looked up with an apologetic look on her face.

Jake's face turned a little bit red; I still hadn't been able to talk to him about his outing with *her* this past Wednesday. He had an indifferent look on his face; I had no idea what he was thinking. I, on the other hand, had just lost my appetite.

"I'm gonna go finish up some homework," Jake said and grabbed his book bag and went into his room.

"Yeah, I'm gonna get started on mine too." I felt bad leaving Aunt Mimi there, with no response to what she just said, but I had nothing good to say! And apparently neither did Jake. This was all so surreal. I threw my book bag on my bed and went to Jake's room down the hall.

"Jake, can I come in?" I knocked on the door and he opened the vault to Pandora's Box. It looked like a tornado had hit.

"Excuse the mess. I wasn't expecting guests." Jake winked and cleared some clothes off his bed so I could have a seat.

"Why, thank you, you don't have to clean for lil' ole me!" Jake looked at me and cocked his head to the side.

"What's up?" Jake asked as if he didn't already know.

"You tell me, we haven't even discussed the fact that *Grace* has graced us with her presence," I said as sarcastically as I could.

"Yeah, I know, it just happened out of nowhere, and bam, two days have gone by." Jake settled down on his desk chair. At least I think that is what it was…it didn't have any books on it. It was packed with DVDs, CDs, and comic books. Jake was a sucker for anything Marvel.

"I am struggling to even look at her, let alone talk to her," I said, hoping Jake would give me some clue about his time with her!

Jake sighed and stared down at the floor.

"I know, I can't lie, at first I was excited to see her. Without a thought, I hopped into the car and went for coffee with her. Uncle Joe came with us and sat at a different table, pretending to read the newspaper. Ya know, I think Uncle Joe observes way more than we give him credit for. Somehow, he knew when I was all done, and he said it was time to go and brought us home."

"How was it? I mean, I'm sorry I acted like such a complete idiot. I'm the older one, and I couldn't even handle it. I should have been there with you." I started to feel bad that he had to fly solo on his first encounter with our estranged mother.

"No worries, we all handle things differently. I fly by the seat of my pants, and you think things through. Put us together and we would be amazing!" Jake said with a smirk, a side smile he learned all too well from our dad.

"Yeah, I guess, I still don't have a clue how to behave around her."

"Just be yourself, Sam. You don't owe her anything. She should be the one stressing, and believe me, she is," Jake said as he raised his eyebrows.

"What do you mean? How was your time out with her?" *Why is he not telling me anything?*

"Well, it was awkward, Sam. I mean, I was six years old when she left. I am practically an adult now," Jake said as though it was a fact. *So funny, he is fourteen and thinks he's an adult, and I feel like I'm acting like a toddler.* "At first we just ordered and sat in silence. She was having a hard time finding the right words to say, I think. She asked about my life here in Big Run, so I told her about sports, my new friends, the church, and how awesome Aunt Mimi and Uncle Joe have been."

"Did she give you any clue as to why she left? Why she never tried to get a hold of us? And why she decided to come back now? I just don't get it." I fired away the questions that have been burning in my brain.

"She didn't get into it really. She did apologize over and over again. I didn't know how to ask those questions. I kinda felt like a deer in headlights. I mean, there I was with my mother, who I never thought I would see again, for years I told myself that she was dead. To think she didn't want to be with us was harder to deal with than death," Jake said, looking up at me for a response.

"I know, I think that is why I'm having such a difficult time with it all. We struggled for a long time after she left. Who knows how life would be if she had never left. Dad wouldn't have lost his job he had back then, and he wouldn't have been traveling on that bridge to work." It was hard not to think about all the things that could have been avoided. It was hard not to ask God why.

"I understand, but 'what if's' only leave me unsatisfied," Jake said with such maturity. He was really growing up into such an awesome person.

"And if I have a brother like you, then who needs her anyway!" I got up and hugged my brother around his neck and kissed him on the cheek. I was so proud of who he was; my dad would have been so proud of how he held his head up high and took each day by storm. We would go through this together. I would be there for him, and he would be there for me. I thanked God that I still had him in my life.

We decided that we would be mature at the dinner table, not for my mother's sake, but for Aunt Mimi and Uncle Joe. They have been so amazing and have treated us as if we were their own. We decided that if they wanted her here for company, we would suck it up and be respectful. Besides, I could smell the roast cooking, and apple pie was for dessert!

....

The knock on the door made my heart skip a beat, not in a good way, but in a nervous way. It was going to be so hard sitting through a meal with that woman and not be sarcastic and rude. I needed some lessons on grace and love from my aunt. She was genuinely happy to see our mother, and my aunt must feel some sort of neglect too. Right? When she chose to leave her family, she affected a lot more than just my dad, my brother, and me. She left everyone that knew her and loved her.

I waited to hear my brother's door open and then I followed behind him. There was Grace, smiling from ear to ear like this was a happy occasion. Did she even know the amount of stress and heartache she was causing just by her very presence? Some people are so selfish they can't see beyond themselves.

I nodded and gave a fake smirk, Jake said hi, and we all sat down at the table. Aunt Mimi was sitting next to Uncle Joe, I was across from them, and Jake was at one end, facing Grace who was at the other end. Aunt Mimi was looking from the woman, to Jake, then to me. She had a look of "are you okay?" on her face. I smiled politely and started serving myself. It never failed my aunt had cooked a feast large enough to feed and army.

"Samantha, why don't you tell your mother about the dance program you are in at the church?" I flashed my aunt a disapproving look. The heat from my face started to rise. How could she call her my mother! I didn't want to tell her anything about my life!

"Oh, Samantha! I am so glad to hear that you have kept up with dancing!" the woman to my right said over enthusiastically.

So how do I respond to that? I wanted to say, Yeah! I am still in dance, you no good piece of crap! *Thanks for remembering that I even took dance! Yippee, Kayay! Should I do some stinkin' pirouettes around the dinner table for you?*

I glanced over at Jake who was giving me that "give her a break" kinda look. Why am I the only one upset here? Why do I feel like the bad guy? Shouldn't she be mortified about her life and the damage that she has done? God please help me understand this!

"Yeah, I'm still in dance, and yeah, they have a program at the church, it's great." I managed to say without looking up.

My aunt wasn't very good at letting silence occur during dinner. So of course she had to go on and on about Jake and how he was the happy little joiner in intramural sports at the school in preparation for next year's baseball and soccer tryouts. Didn't people get it? Sometimes I just want to eat and not have to talk; it's so tiring. And this…this was exhausting! I am not one to pretend or hide how I'm feeling.

"Wow, Jake, that is amazing! I didn't know you were into sports, just like your father," the woman said while slowly bowing her head. Her face was crimson. Was she on crack? I didn't want her to ever reference my father again. He was and still is too good for her.

The rest of dinner was about the same, my aunt trying to push conversation, the woman acting overly excited about everything, my Uncle Joe reserved as usual, and Jake and me giving as little contribution to the convo as we could.

Jake and I respectfully said our good-byes and headed to our rooms as soon as dinner was over. I wanted to hibernate and not see or talk to anyone for a week, for a month, for a year! I didn't want to deal with any of this. I heard the doorbell ring and wondered who the heck else they were expecting?

Knock, knock, knock. "Sam, Jade is here to see you," Aunt Mimi said with her sweet voice.

So much for relaxing and not seeing anyone. I opened the door to see Jade's tear-stained face.

"Hey, sorry for coming here like this without calling. I just didn't know where else to go." Jade plopped down on the floor and started sobbing. Her little belly was starting to emerge even more this past week.

"Hey, girl, it's all good, what is going on?" I immediately got off the bed and sat next to her. Jade sat there crying for a good five minutes before speaking. I became a tissue dispenser.

"I had to leave, I have no one on my side, no one understands." *Sob, sob.* "Except you…" *Sob sob.* "What am I gonna do?" Jade threw her arms around me. I had no idea how I got myself in this position, but here it was. I was the only person Jade felt comfortable with, even though Mariah and Rachel were supportive, they were not checking up on her like I thought they would have. Where are the supportive adults? I was on a mission to get Jade to talk to Gloire; she needed way more guidance than I could give her.

"What happened? Did you have a fight with your parents?" I handed her another Kleenex, and she made sure she was cleaned out before talking again.

"My dad finally broke the silence and asked me flat out what I was planning on doing. I told him I was leaning toward keeping the baby. I told him I didn't know if I could give up my child like that. Well... it didn't go over very well. He got all red in the face, my mother just stood there. I think she thought I was leaning toward adoption. My dad said he didn't support my decision, and I need to make arrangements to live somewhere else." Jade looked down and toward her pile of used Kleenex and picked them up and threw them away. It took her longer to get up; I still could not believe she had a baby in there.

I noticed Jade did not come empty-handed; she had come prepared with a duffel bag.

"Well, I know that Aunt Mimi wouldn't mind if you stayed for the weekend. If you wanted to stay longer, we would have to tell her why. It might not be a bad idea to tell another adult. I was going to ask you if you wanted to talk to Gloire anyways. He has a lot of wisdom." I was hoping she would agree to at least telling someone else that could help her!

Jade took a deep breath, and looked up at me.

"I know, it is going to be quite difficult telling Gloire. He is going to be so disappointed. But I might as well, it's not like I'll be able to hide this secret for long!" Jade pointed at her belly, and we both smiled.

"By the way, who was that pretty woman having tea with Aunt Mimi? She looked like me with tears streaming down her face. I was like, wow, everything fun is happening at your house...oh wait... Oh my gosh, is that her?" I could tell it was sinking in to Jade's brain, just who that was.

"Yeah, it's *her*. My aunt surprised Jake and me when we got home from school that she was coming to dinner—that was a fun meal." The sarcasm was just oozing from me lately.

"Wow, I didn't know that I was ever going to see her. This is nuts. How are you doing? I'm so sorry I just busted in here with all my problems again!" Jade laid her hand on mine and had a horrified look on her face.

"Thanks, but I'm okay. It's not easy. Jake and I are being civil for my aunt and uncle, but all I want to do is tell her to go back where she came from," I said, wondering why the heck that *woman* was crying! It's not like Jake and I were being rude to her! Puhlease, go ahead, cry, cry, cry! I was positive the amount of tears she cried would not even come close to those of my father, Jake, and me. I could feel the blood boiling under my skin.

"Sam, please forgive me. I'm sorry that I brought it up. I didn't mean to make you upset."

"You're fine, it's just…what gives her the right to come in here and boohoo all over my aunt?! I mean, really, doesn't she have someone else she can annoy? I just want her to leave." I was getting myself all worked up, and here was Jade, kicked out of her house, not even knowing where she was going to live. Ugh, it was time to suck it up.

I could tell Jade was biting her tongue.

"Jade, I can see the wheels turning. Tell me what you're thinking."

"Well, do you even know what happened? I mean, why she left? Has anyone been able to find out any information? I mean, until you know exactly what happened…what I'm trying to say is, what if something happened that was beyond her control?" Jade said with sincerity.

"I'm not gonna lie, those thoughts have gone through my head, but seriously, eight years? I think whatever happened, even if she wasn't totally to blame, it is very hard for me to believe that in eight years she couldn't find the time to even make a phone call, write a letter—anything!" The same burning questions that went through my brain on a constant basis.

"Do you think you could ask her? I mean, wouldn't it be good to find out at least, then you can make a decision as to how you want to handle it. I don't know. It might be great to have your mom back in your life, if you could ever forgive her, that is." Jade had a pained look on her face. I could see her brain thinking about her own situation. How she wanted nothing more to be forgiven by her parents. Well, this situation was waaaaay different! How could she possibly compare? I didn't want to get upset with Jade, so I decided to change the subject.

"Well, I am going to ask my aunt if you can stay. I'll be back in flash. Do you want something to drink?" Jade nodded and decided on hot chocolate, *my kinda girl*, and my aunt always had some crazy-flavored gourmet hot chocolate stashed in the cupboard.

I walked out to the kitchen; my aunt and that woman were in deep conversation, and I could tell the woman had been crying. They both looked up at me with hopeful anticipation.

"Aunt Mimi, do you mind if Jade stays the weekend?" I asked, hoping I wouldn't need to explain.

"Sure, no problem, as long as it's okay with her parents," Aunt Mimi said with glossy eyes. Was she crying too? What the heck was going on? Now she's upsetting my aunt? Just go; we don't need you to cause drama here.

I gave her a disapproving glance and proceeded to make the hot chocolates. They were silent, not talking at all. What an awkward feeling that was.

Briiingggg, briiiinnnggg. The telephone rang, and my aunt answered it.

"Hello... Oh, hi, Helena. Why, yes...she is here... um, well, they asked if she could stay the weekend. Yeah, she is safe. Okay, I will let her know." My aunt hung up the phone and glanced over at me with a puzzled look. I could tell I would have to explain, but my aunt was going to wait until the unwelcomed company was gone. My aunt was actually able to pick up on social cues. Why wasn't that *woman*?

"Jade, your mom just called my house. We are going to have to explain things to my aunt later." I handed her a giant mug with the rodent Punxsutawney Phil on it filled with raspberry mocha hot chocolate topped with whipped cream and some cinnamon.

"Ahhhh, this smells delicious, thanks! And yeah, that's fine. We can tell Aunt Mimi. I am getting used to having to disappoint everyone around me."

"Your mom asked if you were safe. your parents love you, Jade, I can tell. I know that this will all work itself out. We just got to pray and get through the bumpy parts for now." I gave her a little squeeze and settled on the area rug next to Jade.

"Thanks, Sam, I hope you're right," Jade said with a smile as she sipped the luscious hot chocolate made by yours truly. Half water, half milk or cream if you have it, topped with whipped cream—mmmmm, not even Aunt Mimi made it this good.

Rumble, rumble. Jades stomach was making god-awful noises that didn't seem human.

"Oh my goodness, how embarrassing. I cannot seem to eat enough lately!" Jade said while patting her small belly.

"Well, you are feeding two. Haha. Let's go fix you a plate of Aunt Mimi's roast, it was delish!" I said while pulling Jade up to her feet. She had already downed the hot chocolate.

"You don't have to twist my arm. I remember Aunt Mimi's cooking, everyone does who experiences it!" Jade said with dancing eyes.

When we went out to the kitchen, my aunt was sitting by herself at the table deep in thought. Uncle Joe was sitting in his rocking chair reading the paper, and Jake was playing his PlayStation 3 with…Gloire! Not sure when he arrived, and not sure when that *woman* left, but was this divine intervention or what?

"Hey, Sam! Jade, is that you?! What's up? Do you girls want to lose in a game of football?" Gloire asked without taking his eyes off the game.

"Aww, gee, no thanks, I have to watch the paint dry," I said in the most sarcastic way possible.

"Yeah, you bet, buddy, I'll take you down!" Jade said with all too much confidence. I remember her telling me that she and her dad played video games together.

"Oh, dems fightin' words, Gloire! I think we have ourselves a duel!" Jake said, retiring his controller to Jade who happily took the challenge.

Gloire and Jade played three stinkin' games of football. Gloire played as the Denver Broncos, and Jade played as the Steelers. It was actually not too bad to watch because of all the bantering going on back and forth, I even caught my Uncle Joe peeking through the paper watching. Aunt Mimi was in the kitchen baking up a storm, but she wasn't saying too much. I was hoping that I could get Aunt Mimi and Gloire alone so Jade could tell them her situation. In the final game, it was neck and neck; Gloire and Jade had each won a game, so this was the tie breaker.

"Touchdown! Wooo hooo, womp there it is!" Jade started doing a victory dance. I hadn't seen Jade this animated, ever. She seemed like a normal high school kid at the moment. Then all of a sudden, she grabbed Gloire by the shirt to keep herself from falling over.

"Hey, kiddo, you all right?" Gloire asked as he helped steady Jade.

"Yeah, I feel a little light-headed right now. Sam, do you think I could have a snack? Jade asked and then it hit me.

"Oh my gosh! I forgot why we even came out here! Aunt Mimi, can we fix Jade a plate of dinner? Oh my goodness, I am so sorry, Jade, I am such a moron."

"Stop it! Don't call yourself names, girl! It's fine, I could have reminded you, my competitive side came out, what can I say?" Jade flashed Gloire a gloating smile.

"Oh please, I was easy on you. You want another go of it? I'll show you whose boss!" Gloire said while he and Jake proceeded to start a new game.

"Gloire, would you like some roast beef, potatoes, carrots, butternut squash, homemade bread, and some apple pie?" Aunt Mimi asked, knowing the answer to her question; she had a coy grin on her face. It didn't take Gloire but two seconds to ditch my brother and the game and make a mad dash for the kitchen table. Gloire immediately started attacking the homemade bread. Everyone in the room had a good belly laugh.

"Ahhhh, Aunt Mimi, you really need to open a restaurant," Gloire said while acting like he was eating his last meal.

"Oh, nonsense, it's just food," Aunt Mimi said while forming a small grin of satisfaction.

Jade and Gloire ate most of what was left, while Jake, Uncle Joe and I picked a little bit at the leftovers. Aunt Mimi was on some sort of baking mission; it smelled amazing, whatever it was.

"I can't eat another bite, oh my Lord!" Gloire said while patting his almost nonexistent belly. He stayed pretty fit with all the sports he played with the youth.

"Tell me about it. I can't breathe." Jade made a bloated face at Gloire.

I was wondering how I could get Gloire and Aunt Mimi alone. How was I going to arrange this?

"Gloire, Aunt Mimi, and Uncle Joe, I have something I need to tell you. I was wondering if you could hear me out for a few minutes. Jake, you can stay too. You are going to hear soon enough, and I would rather you hear it from me anyways." Jade's face was starting to turn red, and she looked at me for support. I nodded my head and smiled, letting her know that this was good. My aunt and uncle joined at the table. Aunt Mimi brought over fresh blueberry and cranberry muffins, coffee, and hot water to make tea. She was the best hostess I had ever known.

Jake looked at me with a puzzled expression. Gloire had his hands folded in front of him on the table, looking intently at Jade. Aunt Mimi and Uncle Joe were fixing themselves some coffee and tea, and I was praying as hard as I could for Jade at the moment. How many awkward moments was she going to have over the next couple of months? My heart went out to her.

"Well, I don't know how else to say this, but to just say it. I was in a relationship with a boy a few months ago, and I went way further than I should have. I am now twelve weeks pregnant, and my parents want me to give the baby up for adoption, and we are not in agreement." Jade was speaking matter-of-factly, then all of a sudden, her voice started to falter. "My father thinks that would be a bad influence on my sister, and he has asked me to make other living arrangements." Jade took a deep breath and stared down at the floor. No one said anything for a few moments. Jake's face turned red from embarrassment. What did he have to be embarrassed for?

"Jade, when you say that you are not in agreement, what does that mean?" Gloire asked ever so carefully.

"I want to keep it, at least now I do. I just can't imagine giving away my child. I know that adoption is good for when a person isn't fit to be a parent. But that is not me. I know I can do this with support." Jade looked at Gloire, pleading for his agreement with her.

"Jade, I will help you with anything that you need. We all make mistakes, we all fall short. But God's mercy and grace is never ending, and I am proud of you that you believe that you can do this. I know that you can. First, we need to find a place for you to stay in the meantime. Would you be willing to have a meeting with your parents, Katie, and myself if I set it up?" Gloire asked with kind and gentle eyes. Where did these people come from? He said he was proud of her? At that moment, I wanted to cry of happiness and hug the heck out of Gloire.

Aunt Mimi and Uncle Joe exchanged looks. "She is welcome to stay with us as long as she needs to. Jade, you are welcome here. Although I will need to have a conversation with your mom so she understands that I am not stepping on their toes, I am just providing a place for you while you guys sort this out."

"Thank you so much, all of you." Jade was trembling now and crying of relief. I couldn't hold it in any longer. Tear were streaming down my face. I was so relieved for her.

Gloire got up and went over to her and laid hands on her shoulders.

"God, we thank You for Jade. We thank You for Your grace and Your mercy. You see her repentant heart and her faithfulness to take care of the life inside of her. We ask that You would give her wisdom and strength in the days ahead, we ask for Your provision. God, we come before You and ask for reconciliation between Jade and her family. We know that You are a

God of restoration. We thank You ahead of time for the miracle that You are going to do in her family. We also ask for you to bless this house. We ask for You to provide above and beyond the needs of the Anderson's and their family. We love you, God. We ask this in the mighty name of Jesus. Amen."

"Amen!" Aunt Mimi said while raising her fist in the air. She loved to pray, and when people prayed with authority like Gloire, it made her all the more excited.

Gloire, Jade, and I continued to talk. Jade told him everything about school and what was going on with her ex-boyfriend and his new girlfriend. Aunt Mimi called Helena and was on the phone with her for a while. Uncle Joe and Jake set up the air mattress in my room and brought out all the blankets like she did when Kate came for a visit.

11

Meetings of the Heart

Gloire got a phone call after Jade's confession, and he flew out the door at 11:30 p.m. without even a word! Jade and I were worried. We sat up and talked almost through the night. We got a phone call around 8:00 a.m. that Katie had her baby! It was two weeks early, but it was perfectly healthy. We could not wait to go and see the baby. Aunt Millie drove us to the hospital immediately. We brought flowers for Katie, a stuffed bear for baby Daniel, and a favorite drink from the One Way Café for Gloire. Gloire was beaming from ear to ear, and Katie was one string away from passing out; the poor girl had to endure company after such suffering. Ugh, I could not imagine squeezing a watermelon through a kiwi! *It should be illegal to visit someone the same day they deliver.* Jade held that baby and locked eyes with Katie. It was apparent that Katie was going to be a huge help to Jade in the days to come.

After we left, we went back home to go back to sleep. We were mentally and physically exhausted. My eyes were screaming for me to shut them, and I was glad to oblige. These past couple of months had been a roller coaster. All I knew is, I was along for the ride. I could hear Jade snoring in my bed. I took the air mattress; even though it is comfortable, its way harder to get in and out of than my bed. For Jade, moving isn't as easy right at the moment, and it's only going to get worse.

My mind could not stop thinking about all the changes. My life was so different; I wouldn't even recognize it going back three months ago. The holidays were around the corner, and I was getting nervous about how I was going to feel. For Christmas with my dad, it was just us. Quiet, cozy, and full of yummy food, gifts, hot chocolate, movie marathons, Stratego, Uno, fuzzy pants, and lots of couch time. Dad would take a full week of work off, and we would spend it all together. Jake and I barely hung out with our friends during that week; we were so content chillin' at home with dad; my eyes were getting heavy reminiscing all the great memories. I was hoping to end up in a dream where I could see my dad once again.

....

"Sam, Jade, are you guys going to get up today? It's almost four o'clock!" I could hear Aunt Mimi tapping on the door.

Well, if I did plan on sleeping through the day, that plan was destroyed.

"Yes, Aunt Mimi, getting up," I said with a groggy voice.

"Wow, I could have slept even longer. I can't believe it's 4:00 p.m," Jade said as she fixed her dark ponytail and wiped the sleep from her eyes.

I could smell a giant brunch coming through the crevices of my door. It's puzzling that I had not gained weight eating all this rich comfort food my aunt made on a daily basis. My only saving grace was the fact that I danced, and the healthy breakfast and lunches I ate every day at school.

The weekend ended with a powerful message at church. It was one on forgiveness and God's everlasting mercy. Very similar to what Gloire prayed over Jade on Friday night. Jade's parents were both at church; it was very awkward at first. Aunt Mimi and Uncle Joe went out for coffee after service with them. Afterward her father came to the house and asked Jade to come back home. Jade was hesitant at first, but when she saw the softness of his eyes, she ran into his arms. I know it was selfish, but I was jealous for that moment. I was trying to remember the last hug that I had with my dad. I wished that I could hug him one last time.

Thanksgiving came fast, and we spent it with just the four of us for dinner. What. A. Spread. I felt guilty having so much to eat! Jade and her family came over for dessert. It was so great seeing the family in happy conversation around the table. Jade's father said that he was thankful for having such a strong daughter; none of the women at the table had a dry eye.

I had practice with Ms. Yvonne on Monday, and my dance solo for fine arts was coming along great. In the group, we were working on the Christmas play, and Saturday rehearsals were scheduled with the drama team from now until Christmas. I looked forward to every practice. I missed the dance studio at the School of the Arts, but I have to say I wasn't missing out on dance instruction. I was learning a new way to move my body and to use every emotion I was feeling and put it into my dance. I knew that is what you are supposed to do, but I could never tap into what I am tapping into now. Maybe it was my dad passing, or my mother resurfacing; whatever it was, it was helping me to become a better dancer. The music that we were dancing to had more meaning to me than any other music I had ever used. Ms. Yvonne said that the music had anointing. It meant that God was using it to touch people's hearts. The dance was God inspired—that I knew for sure.

Wednesday morning, I needed coffee. I had such a hard time sleeping the night before. I had a dream, or should I say nightmare, that my mother was going to the same church, and she was sitting right next to me smiling away and happy as clam. *Why the heck is a clam happy?* Anyways, lunchtime could not come soon enough.

"Sam, what the heck? Where have you been all my life?" Sam grabbed my head and put me in a headlock.

"You know you are such a gentleman!" I said, punching him playfully in the stomach while he pretended to fall over.

"Seriously where have you been? I miss our coffee chats," he said with a wink.

"Yeah, I know, it has been crazy. I do want to get together with you." I sat down and looked around waiting for Mariah, Rachel, Pat, and Jade. "Where is everyone?"

"They should be coming soon. Jade had her locker vandalized or something this morning, I don't know who, why, or how!" Sam said with a puzzled expression while he dug into his ginormous lunch bag.

I had a sick feeling in my stomach; I looked over to the table where those "lovely" girls sat, the ones who confronted Jade last week. They were looking in our direction and laughing.

"Man, am I so ready to eat. I'm starving!" Mariah said as she and Rachel sank into their chairs and dropped their bags on the ground.

"Tell me about it, this day had better turn around!" Rachel said as she started putting together her salad.

I looked at Mariah with a questioning glance. I needed to know that Jade was okay.

"Well, Jade won't be joining us today. She has a meeting that she set up." Mariah looked at me with the "you already know the details" kind of look.

"Ohhh, that's right, It's Wednesday," I said, remembering that Jade had a meeting set up with Ms. Rose and her parents.

"You girls are weird. Anyway, I'm getting an ice cream, does anyone need anything?" Sam asked as he got up and immediately slammed his body into Pat who had just arrived. They almost knocked over Rachel's salad. Her indignant face made them laugh while they headed up to the lunch line.

"Okay, please tell me what the heck is going on, Jade's locker was vandalized? I don't get it. Who would do that?" Well, I *obviously* knew who it probably was, but I didn't want to accuse before I knew.

"*Oh*, yeah, did Sam tell you? Oh my goodness, we got off the bus and walked to our lockers just like every other morning. But today, Jade had the word THOT—*that ho over there*—painted in huge red letters all the way down her locker. She was so embarrassed. We missed first period washing it off."

"What did the principal say? Do you know who did it? How did Jade take it?"

"Well, we have our suspicions!" Rachel said as she folded her arms and glanced over to the table where Jade's ex-boyfriend's new girlfriend sat.

"Yeah, it probably was. They have been looking over here quite often and laughing. Whatever, Jade doesn't need this crap right now." I was wondering how much more this poor girl was going to be able to take.

Sam and Pat came back, so we stopped our conversation. They didn't know anything about Jade yet, but that was not our business to tell.

I could not stop thinking about Jade all afternoon. I was wondering how she was doing, how the meeting went with her parents, and just plain old missing my friend. I wished more than ever that I had a cell phone and could at least text her and know that she was okay.

Youth group was fun tonight. Sam, Mariah, Rachel, Pat, Jake, and his friend Tom, and I were in a group and we had to come up with five things we would bring on a deserted island that were no bigger than the size of our hands. We had to collectively work as a team and come up with a way that those five things would help us get off the island and return home. The lady who coordinates the drama team helped Gloire run the meeting. It was a blast. We came in second place for survival and won free movie passes! Score!

Jade never showed up to Amped on Wednesday night. I was really starting to get worried. I tried calling her when I got home, and no one answered. I was having a hard time sleeping, so I started counting sheep, but they kept landing on each other, and then I started laughing at myself. Pathetic. I decided to read my Bible. For some reason, I opened to Mathew 18:21. It talked about how many times we were to forgive. Jesus answered and said seventy times seven! And in one day! The same offense! I could not believe what I was reading. How is that even possible? I had a Study Bible that my dad gave me one year for Christmas. It had other scriptures that talked about forgiveness. It says if we don't forgive, God can't forgive us! It made me mad. There are just some things that aren't forgivable right? I mean, does God really expect me to forgive my mother? Forget about sleep; my mind was now spinning even more.

....

Sleepless nights and I do not get along; I was like a zombie throughout the entire day. I tripped three times, dropped my coffee all over my favorite faded purple American Eagle hoodie, fell asleep during English, my favorite subject, and I missed the bus home because I had to stay after school to make up for my siesta during English! My Uncle Joe had to come and get me.

"I'm so sorry, Uncle Joe, I had quite a day. I am so sorry that I let my slobbery sleepy mess make you have to come out here to get me," I said as I climbed into his pick-up truck. Uncle Joe smiled and winked at me.

"So how is school going? Besides today of course," Uncle Joe said while raising and lowering his eyebrows. Was I really going to have a conversation that lasted more than thirty seconds with Uncle Joe?

"It's actually going pretty good. I have decent grades," I said while thinking about how I never got a chance to talk to Jade today, besides a flyby in the hallway. She was at school, but she went straight to the counselor's office for lunch. She told me she would call me later. She looked like she was in good spirits, and that is really all that mattered to me.

"Well, that's good to hear." Uncle Joe was concentrating on the road, like he always did. He made it his business to make sure that we were safe. I could feel it in everything that he did.

"Uncle Joe, can I ask you a question?" I asked, looking at his salt-and-pepper beard, loving the way each strand seemed to meet white and dark perfectly.

"Shoot," Uncle Joe said, welcoming conversation.

"I was reading the Bible last night, in Matthew 18. There was a verse that said that we had to forgive everyone, and if we don't forgive those that have hurt us, God won't forgive us."

Uncle Joe started rubbing his meticulously manicured beard. "Well, what's your question?" he said, not deterring his focus from the construction up ahead.

"Well, is that true in all cases? What about all the horrible things people do? Are we supposed to forgive them too? What if they are not sorry? I just don't get it. It doesn't seem fair!"

Uncle Joe pulled into a little diner shaped like a submarine called The Watering Hole. It didn't seem like an appetizing name.

"Let's grab a drink and have a chat," Uncle Joe said as he parked next to another beat-up pickup truck. I was glad I was with Uncle Joe, but this didn't look too promising; anyhow, I was really excited to talk to Uncle Joe.

Uncle Joe ordered coffee, black, with a large slice of grape pie. I ordered a large chocolate milkshake and bowl of oatmeal. The waitress looked at me strange. Probably a weird thing for a teenager to order. I loved oatmeal. I loved putting all kinds of fruits and nuts in it; my dad always said I was an inspiration for him to eat healthier. It took Uncle Joe a few minutes to speak again. He looked outside and observed his truck, the people in the diner, and he started to inspect the booth we were in. You would think he was a detective in his former life.

"Well, where were we, kiddo? You want to know about forgiveness, eh?" Uncle Joe said, taking a slow careful sip of his coffee.

I was sucking down the milkshake like it was my business to; man, was it good! The inside looked like an old fifties diner that never changed. And I believe that is exactly what it was. It wasn't dirty or broken, but the décor was old, antique-ish, but not horrifying for some reason. It made me think of what it would be like if I ever was able to visit my grandparents, if I had ever gotten a chance to go to their house.

"Yeah, I had a hard time sleeping after reading that last night," I said, taking a giant mouthful of oatmeal.

It had walnuts and brown sugar on the top. It was fantastic, definitely made with milk and not water.

"How so? Why is this bothering you so much?" my uncle asked, although I believe he knew the answer; he was just waiting for me to say it.

"Well, as you know, it's been very difficult having Grace come back. I feel anger every time I see her. I don't know if I'll ever be able to forgive her for what she did, and now, I won't be forgiven?"

Uncle Joe took a few more sips and another bite of his pie before answering. I was getting anxious.

"Let me ask you this, why did you have to stay after school again?"

I had no idea why he was asking me this. "I had a rough night of sleep, so…I kinda fell asleep in English class. My teacher was not too happy with me."

"Oh, I see. What did he say after school?" Uncle Joe was now completely focused on me.

"Well, he told me to make sure that I got a good night's rest tonight, and that wasn't a good-enough excuse to fall asleep in his class. He said that I was one of his best students, and he didn't want to see my grades slip."

"Okay, well, how was he with you after you explained to him why you fell asleep?" Uncle Joe said while finishing the last bite of his pie and motioning to the waitress for more coffee.

"Well, at first he was upset because it wasn't like my character, but after I explained, he was fine. He said that he was proud of the work that I was handing in and that he loved to hear my perspective on different literary pieces."

"So would you say that he forgave you? Uncle Joe asked and looked me dead in the eyes. Now I knew where he was going with this.

"Well, yes, he did! But Uncle Joe, that is *not* the same thing! I mean really, falling asleep in class…you can't compare that to abandoning your family!"

I was getting more outraged by the second! Did he really want to compare that to what my *mother* did?

"Sam, I am not comparing them. I am just trying to show you that God is good. His grace is for everyone. It is His desire to be reconciled with all of His children. You did something to your teacher that offended him. When he heard your explanation, he was forgiving. He had grace for you. He even complimented you in a time when you were being punished. What if he didn't forgive you? How do you think the rest of the school year would be?"

I sat there, trying to comprehend what was being said. I got what he was saying, but it still didn't diminish the fact that they are two separate things.

"I get what you're saying, but still, they are two extremely different scenarios."

"Sam, do you know why your mother left?" Uncle Joe asked carefully.

"No, you know that I don't," I said with a bit of irritation in my voice.

Uncle Joe looked at me while folding his gently used napkin. He seemed way too careful about things to be a rugged farmer.

"Did you ever think that maybe you should find out, that is, before you decide to forgive her or not?" Uncle Joe asked very simply.

"Yeah, I have thought about finding out, but how? How do I approach that? Don't you think that she should be coming to me?" I said and leaned back into the red-colored cushioned booth and folded my arms.

Uncle Joe scratched his beard and looked outside to check on his truck again; it was convenient that we were sitting by the window.

"Have you given her opportunity to explain? I think she may be waiting for the right time, when you are ready to hear her. I think she may be giving you time to process her return." Uncle Joe said like he had inside information. It still didn't help the fact that I felt like I was in the firing squad right now. Well, I wanted to talk to Uncle Joe, and I sure got an earful!

"Can I share a story with you?" Uncle Joe asked, probably seeing the expression of hurt on my face.

"Shoot," I said.

Uncle Joe smiled. "Well, I want to give you a little background on your aunt and me. I had my sight set on your aunt when I was twelve years old. There was no one else I wanted to be with. Your aunt did not feel the same. Boy did she make me work for it! It wasn't until I was eighteen years old and helping your grandfather run the farm that she paid any attention to me. But when she did, it wasn't even six months later that we were married."

I could tell my uncle loved my aunt so much, just watching the expression on his face told me that he loved her now, just as he did back then, if not even more than when they were young.

"Wow, that's a long time Uncle Joe, you got married so young!" I could not imagine being married two years from now, it's amazing how fast things change.

"Yeah, we are going on thirty-five years! It still seems like yesterday, though. Life wasn't easy as a young, married couple. We had to grow up together. Your aunt had gotten a job at the bakery in town, and we were trying to make ends meet. I was working on the farm and stocking at the grocery store. On one particular day, I got out of work a bit early and stopped at a local bar to grab a drink before I picked up your aunt from work. Back then, I used to relax by having a few drinks. It helped me calm down from a hard day's work. It wasn't the best idea I had. Before I knew it, I had too much to drink, and when I went to pick up your aunt, I still wasn't sober. Your aunt hadn't learned to drive yet, so I put on the best face I could so she wouldn't be mad at me for drinking too much. We were on our way home when I swerved to miss a deer, which I did in fact miss, but when I tried to pull the car back into position, I lost control and hit a tree on your aunt's side of the car. The impact was great enough that both of us were knocked out. We were lucky that someone saw us and sent for help. We are lucky to be alive."

"Wow, Uncle Joe that is crazy! I'm so glad that God protected the both of you! I mean, look at you. Neither of you look like you were in an accident like that," I said, having a hard time processing my uncle drinking too much. I had never seen him drink like that.

Uncle Joe was looking at me with very sad eyes. He was fiddling with his napkin again, only with nervous hands.

"Well, you're right we were protected. Your aunt and I. When I woke up at the hospital, I ran to find your aunt to make sure she was okay. She was still out when I saw her. She looked like an angel sleeping. When she woke up, she saw me and we hugged and cried. The doctor came in and said except a few small cuts and bruises we were fine. But then the news came that we were not prepared for. Your aunt had been pregnant, and we didn't even know it. With the impact of the car hitting the tree and your aunt's body being tossed about, we lost the baby." Uncle Joe stared down at his coffee cup rubbing the handle with his thumb.

I didn't even know what to say. I always wondered why my aunt and uncle never had kids. *Why didn't they try again?*

"I was so ashamed that my one bad decision caused my wife, the woman I loved more than any other human on the planet, grief that could never be reversed. We tried to have kids several times. Something happened during the accident with your aunt's reproductive organs, and she had complications. She was never able to carry a child to term. Your aunt has had three other miscarriages. After the last one, we decided to stop. It was too painful. Your mom had come to live with us after your grandpa passed, so we raised her as if she was our own. Your aunt, your amazing aunt, forgave me when I had no business of being forgiven. It took years for me to forgive myself. It is only by the grace of God that your aunt was able to forgive me and love me the way that she does. Don't you see? We don't deserve God's grace. When we decide to not offer it to someone else, it makes a mockery of what Jesus did for us on the cross." My uncle was looking at me with sympathetic eyes.

I had to wipe the tears from my face; the story was so tragic. My beautiful aunt, what a great mother she would have been; I mean what a great mother she is!

"Uncle Joe, I think I understand what you are saying, I'm just not there yet. I am so sorry that you were not able to have kids. You would have been a great father, and Aunt Mimi, geez…I cannot think of anyone who would be better at raising kids than her," I said, having a hard time controlling my tears.

"Ahhh, but don't you see God's redemption? Your aunt got to raise your mother. Their relationship is that of a mother and daughter. And then we have become doubly blessed having you and Jake. I can't get your aunt to stop baking, and cooking! She is beside herself with joy every day because the two of you are here with us. She was shocked when your father named us as legal guardians. You two have filled our home with joy."

I was now crying pretty good; so much so that the waitress came over and gave my uncle extra napkins. When I looked up, Uncle Joe was wiping tears from his eyes.

Uncle Joe paid the bill, and he had his arm around me as we walked to the car. I leaned my head into his chest as we walked, just like I did with my dad. I felt more at home at that moment than I had since I left NYC.

When we got home, my aunt flashed my uncle a disapproving glance. You could see that she had been worried. I wasn't even aware of the time, but dinner was ready. My uncle and I had been at the diner for nearly two hours. I had so much to process I couldn't even think about eating. However, I managed a few bites to satisfy my aunt. I could not stop thinking about what my uncle had told me. I wanted to hug my aunt and tell her what an amazing person she was. If only I could be like that. Would I ever be able to give grace like that? It would have to be supernatural, because I know I could not do that on my own.

12

Grace, Grace, God's Grace

Uncle Joe's words never left my mind. All weekend long, I couldn't concentrate on anything else. I met Sam out for coffee, and he could tell my mind was on other things. I finally told him everything about my mother, about Uncle Joe and Aunt Mimi. We prayed together, and he promised he would keep me in prayer about my mother. I said I would pray for his family and his sister Victoria who was getting herself into trouble ever since their mother passed.

I spent the night at Jade's house on Saturday. Her family was meeting regularly with Ms. Rose. They were going to support Jade's decision to keep the baby. Her father had even started turning their spare bedroom into a nursery. Jade was looking much more healthy, and her family seemed normal again. I was so happy for her. They had decided that she would go to school until she was really showing, then she was going to go into a program where she only had to go to school three hours a day, and she would finish the year early, before she had the baby. Helena was going to change her hours at work so Jade could finish her senior year at our high school next year. Everything was set into place for her. I decided not to burden her with everything I was going through. I was realizing that the more I talked to God about things, the better I was able to handle them.

Getting ready for Sunday church at Jade's was easy; she had her own bathroom! I had a nervous pit in my stomach, and I didn't know why.

We didn't make it to Sunday school, so when I got to church Aunt Mimi hugged me like I had been gone for years.

"Oh, Sam, you look so beautiful!" Aunt Mimi said as she gave me big kiss on the cheek. I had on a black skirt, striped leggings, a blue fitted long sleeved T-shirt, long black boots, and a matching cashmere scarf. I'm not gonna lie; raiding Jade's closet was pretty fun.

"Thanks, Aunt Mimi." I smiled and returned her big hug and kiss. I made it about halfway down the aisle before I stopped dead in my tracks. My heart started to beat pretty fast, and I made my way into a seat to the right of the pulpit. Jade followed me, and when she saw the look on my face, she followed my gaze.

"Oh my goodness, Sam, is that your mother?" she asked with a concerned voice.

"Yep, it is," I said, remembering the dream that I had a while back.

The youth group usually sits up front. I didn't want to pass her at the moment.

"Sam, Jade, what the heck? Why are you sitting all the way back here? Get up, come on sit with us!" Mariah said. There was no telling Mariah and Sam no. They pulled both Jade and me up to the second row from the front. Jake was already sitting down; he looked up at me reading my mind.

Worship was really good. I was able to really focus on God and not let all the other things around me get in the way. The youth were spread out in front of the altar with Gloire, praying and worshipping.

The pastor got up to the pulpit, and his face was beet-red.

"God's presence is here, people! If you have a need today, if you need forgiveness, if you need healing, He is here! If the elders could please come up, we are going to pray with you, for whatever need you have. Don't worry about who is next to you or who is behind you, God wants to touch you today. Please don't miss an opportunity to meet with God."

People started crowding toward the altar. Out of the corner of my eye, I saw my mother go up. Tears were streaming down her face. Shortly after my aunt met her at the front, they both fell down to their knees and hugged each other, crying. One of the elders prayed for my mother, and she started shaking and sobbing. My heart started pounding, just like the time it did in Amped when I knew God was calling me, when I gave my heart to God. Something in me was wanting to run up to the front. I didn't know what to do. My soul was screaming for me to move, and my head was saying no way! My heart started beating so fast; I was sure everyone around me was able to hear it. I got up, moved out of the row, and walked forward. I felt like I was in slow motion. I couldn't hear anything around me. I thought I had gone deaf for a moment. Then I heard a voice.

"Sam, I am going to restore what you have lost." I looked around; there was no one talking to me. Could this be God's voice? I just couldn't believe it. It was like He was right here. I could audibly hear it. If there were any doubts of the pounding in my heart, hearing voices topped the chart. Without any hesitation, I knelt down behind my mother and my aunt. My hands were shaking, but I managed to put my left hand on the small of my mother's back. I could feel heat coming from her like I had never experienced before. Shortly after, I felt a hand on my back, then two more. Before long, I had more hands on me than I could count. I opened my eyes, and my brother was sitting next to me. He was praying out loud. I had never heard him pray before. He was praying for me. I lost it. My precious brother was praying for my heart to be healed. Where did this kid come from? I gave into the Spirit that was prompting me and felt a release like I had never experienced in my life. Suddenly I felt light; I felt like I was defying gravity, and they were going to have to tie me down.

My mother shifted her position and turned to see who was behind her. We locked eyes. She had a look of utter shock and disbelief in her eyes. She gently moved the hair from my watery eyes and slowly put out her arms to see if I would allow her to hug me. I slowly moved forward. My mother wrapped her arms around me so tightly; I felt like I was four years old with a large blanket tucked in all directions, keeping me safe and warm. We cried. I grabbed Jake and pulled him in. I don't know how long we were there, but it felt like eternity, and no time at all. We were there long after the pastor dismissed the congregation. When we finally got up, it was a little awkward. We all took turns with the tissue box. Aunt Mimi invited my mother back to the house for supper. She accepted. I was feeling a bit nervous. I really didn't know what just happened, but I think that I just forgave my mother. The funny thing was, I still had no idea what her excuse was as to why she left in the first place. For some reason, it didn't matter. After the discussion I had with my uncle, I came to the realization that forgiving someone doesn't just release them, it releases you. Today I had experienced what grace really was. It's undeserving, it's overflowing, and it's never out of reach. I still had so many questions and so much I needed to learn.

After dinner, Jake and I agreed to go out for coffee with our mother. We rode in her old Buick Lacrosse. It was loud, and I felt like I was in some sort of hillbilly scene from a movie, but it was no movie; this was reality. We rode in silence. I don't think any of us knew how to start the conversation.

The One Way Café was closed on Sunday, so we had to settle for the diner in town. The coffee wasn't as good, but the place wasn't half bad for a diner, and it was almost empty. Good for a private conversation.

"Hi, Grace, ughhhhh, you wouldn't believe the crazy couple that just left. You should be thankful you requested off on Sundays, you should see the type of riffraff we get in here!" an older waitress with frown lines said as she prepared for our orders.

Apparently, this was her new place of employment. Why would she want to work here? Did that mean she was going to stay here? Too many questions were running rampant in my brain.

"Hi, Betty, um yeah, I am not going to be working here on Sundays at all from now on," my mother said as her face turned a shade of red.

"Well, good for you, dear, what can I get you, folks?" she said as she tried her best to smile through her cigarette-stained teeth.

We all ordered a dessert and a hot beverage. It took a minute before anyone spoke up.

"Thank you for coming out with me. You can't understand how much I appreciate this," my mom said as she put cream in her coffee.

"Who was that lady? You work here? How and when did that happen?" Well, Jake had no problem getting information. He didn't overthink things the way that I tended to do.

"Well, that woman was the only one who would hire me in this town. I wanted to be close…and well, it is very convenient to where I am staying right now," my mother said as she took a careful sip of her coffee. It was hard not to stare at her. She was so beautiful. My dad could never say it enough, how beautiful she was, and how she defied age. She still looked like she could be my older sister. I remember him telling her that all the time when we were little. When I was little, people thought she was still in her older teenage years!

"Oh, well, where are you staying?" Jake asked with a moustache of whipped cream that came off the top of his hot chocolate.

My mother hesitated for a moment, stirring her coffee. "Well, actually I am staying at Angels of Mercy right now," she said, quickly glancing from Jake then to me.

That was the name of the charity that our church raised money for, the women and children that were rescued from human trafficking. Why was my mother there? Was she helping them out?

"Oh, nice, did they hire you, or are you volunteering?" I was really interested in how the heck she got involved so quickly!

My mother leaned back in her chair and folded her arms neatly in her lap and looked at me with sad eyes. Jake was making slurping noises with his drink; I wasn't sure if it was out of nervousness or just the fact that he is a boy.

"Well, I am not volunteering right now, I hope to in the future. But for right now, I am actually going through their program as a participant." My mother let out a large sigh.

A participant? What was she talking about? I was so confused. She must have noticed the look on my face, and then she proceeded to tell Jake and me what we had been dying to know for eight years.

"Sam, Jake, I need to tell you what happened to me. I want to apologize for not coming to you sooner, I was ashamed." My mother lowered her head and closed her eyes for a split second; I assumed she was saying a quick prayer. "Well, your father and I got married at a very young age. We really didn't get the chance to explore the world before we were up to our ears in diapers and bills. I now look back on the diapers and bills years as the greatest times in my life," my mother said and chuckled as if off in a distant thought. "Anyways, after Jake started preschool, I had time on my hands for the first time in years. I couldn't wait to get out into the world and make something of myself! I started working at the bakery. Remember the one down on the corner?"

Jake and I just shook our heads in agreement. "Well, I thought I was going to open my own bakery/coffee shop someday. I started hanging out with one of the other bakers. She was close to my age. Your father didn't like her too much and warned me to not get too close. Well, he was right. Before I knew it, I was hanging out with her almost every weekend. It started out just innocent, going to hear bands play and having a few drinks. After a while, I didn't care what I was doing while I was out. I started using drugs. It affected everything around me. I started forgetting to get you from school because I was passed out, or high. Your father was worried that I would hurt one of you guys, and he told me to leave and get myself cleaned up and come back when I was ready to be a wife and mother again. Well, I did leave." Now there were tears starting to form in the corners of my mother's eyes. "At first, I went to the hospital and tried to check myself in. They told me my insurance didn't cover rehab, and I wasn't a big enough threat to be admitted. So I stayed with my friend for a while. One night we were out, and we met a group of guys at the bar. They wanted us to go to a party with them. My friend and I were already drunk and high, so we went along with them. We never made it to the party. These men gagged us and threw us in the back of a van and drove for days. I didn't even know where I was for weeks. They sold us to a ring of rich men that paid for women, women they could do whatever they wanted to." My mother paused for a moment; she had a sad look on her face. "My friend was very feisty and tried to escape, spitting in the faces of these men. They put a bullet in her head right in front of me. I knew then that if I wanted to live, I had to do what they asked."

My mother was now trying to control her tears. I didn't know what to say or how to react. My stomach was sick. I looked at Jake who was frowning and slowly shaking his head back and forth.

"I spent five years in Chicago, in the center of this drug and sex trafficking ring. I wanted to die, but what I wanted even more than death was to see my husband and my children again."

My mother put her face in her hands and cried. Jake and I didn't move; we were both in shock. After a minute or so, my mother continued in a shaky voice

"Another girl and I talked about escaping so many times. We had no money, and we knew no one that would help us. I tried a couple of times, while I was with…while I was with an um…patron…begging them to help. It was no use, they only ended up telling those wretched men who 'owned' us, and well, we suffered the consequences. It wasn't until they thought I was too old that I was finally able to be free. I was penniless, homeless, and so ashamed. I should have come home, but I had gotten myself into the situation. Me, I did it to myself. If only I would have listened to your father." My mother looked away, not able to look Jake and me in the face.

I adjusted my chair and moved it closer to my mom—my mom, who went through hell and whom I held hostage in my mind and in my actions, adding to the confinement that she had endured for years. "I really don't even know what to say. All this time…all this time, I was so angry with you. I was so mad that you left your family and never tried to contact us. And you were stolen. You were taken away from us!" I put my face in my hands and cried just like my mother, for my mother, for me, for Jake, and most of all, for my dad. My daddy—he never knew what really happened.

My mother put her hand on my shoulder and spoke to Jake and me. "I am so sorry that my selfishness stole years away from the both of you. Do you think you would ever be able to forgive me?"

Jake put his arms around my mother, and I knew that he had already forgiven her. I looked her directly in the eye.

"I already did…Mom…today in church. God showed me what grace was. He is teaching me so much. You don't have to apologize. I know that you are sorry. I know that you made it right with God today. It wouldn't be right for me to hold that against you. I am sorry for the way that I treated you when you came back. I didn't even give you a chance to explain. Will you forgive me?" I asked through a quivering voice.

My mother grabbed my neck and hugged both Jake and me until the strain was hurting my joints! We spent the rest of our time talking about life with Dad and our new life here. My mother had plans to help out with The Angels of Mercy ministry. They not only help rescue woman and children who have been affected by human trafficking; they sew dresses and ship them overseas for missionaries to distribute to woman who have been trafficked in India and Africa. My mother seemed very passionate about it. She also had plans to establish herself here in Big Run, and when and if we were ready, she wanted us to live together and have a chance as a family again.

The week flew by; my mother was at my aunt's house every day. I could not wait to see my mom when I got home from school; she was there. She wanted to hear every word that I had to say.

....

We had a Christmas Eve service at the church. Our Christmas production was a hit! I felt like the whole town was there to support us. During my dance solo, there was one point where I faced forward in third position with my hand extended upward toward heaven. I saw my mother looking at me with tears streaming down her face. It was so hard to hold it together. After our Christmas production, Ms. Yvonne gave me a huge hug and reminded me about the fine arts competition over April break. My mother overheard and offered to help chaperone during the trip. My heart skipped a beat. I could not believe how far we had come in just a few weeks.

My mother stayed the night at our house on Christmas Eve. But when I woke up Christmas morning, the air mattress was empty, and the blankets were folded up neatly and placed in the corner of the room. I started to panic. Did she leave? Is she gone already? It was Christmas morning! I was so scared to open my door and not see her there. I didn't think I could take that type of heartbreak again.

I slowly walked out into the hall. I could smell bacon cooking and waffles or pancakes of some sort. Aunt Mimi had probably been up for hours already, making sure we have one heck of a Christmas breakfast. I slowly turned the corner to see my aunt *and* my mom, busily running around the kitchen working together. Music was softly playing, and my mother was humming. She looked up at me and a huge smile formed across her face.

"Merry Christmas, beautiful! Hot chocolate? Coffee? OJ? What can I get you to drink?" she hustled over to me and wrapped her arms around me. I started to cry.

"Honey, what's the matter? Are you okay?" My mom pulled back and wiped the tears from my eyes. I felt like a three-year-old. *Come on, Sam, get it together!*

"Yes, I'm fine. I just woke up and saw the blankets folded, and I didn't hear you get up…and well."

"Sam, I am not going anywhere! You are not going to be able to get rid of me, I give you my word." And with that, my mother pulled me in for a long hug. Aunt Mimi took over humming, while my mother fixed me a café mocha. After a short conversation on the phone with Kate-wishing each other Merry Christmas, it was time to celebrate as a family.

The tree was overloaded with gifts. I didn't even know what to think. It took us an hour and a half to open everything. My aunt and uncle bought Jake and me both cell phones. I cried. Yup, not to sound like a cliché teenager, but I cried over a phone. My mother went a little crazy on us. I got tons of new clothes, dance outfits, and new dance shoes. The best present was a box. Jake and I both received shoeboxes from my mother. When we opened it, it was jampacked with letters. Some written on napkins, paper, even cardboard that comes out of the packages of stockings. My mother never missed a birthday, Christmas, Easter, Valentine's Day, and just any old day she felt like writing to us. Even in her darkest hour and imprisoned life, she never forgot. I was so overcome with emotions I couldn't speak for what seemed like eternity.

It was the perfect day. The love that we now felt for each other was not just a love for an aunt, an uncle, brother, sister, mother, or daughter. It was love that was intertwined with the love that God lavishes on us. It was grace, it was mercy, it was unconditional, and it was at our fingertips.

Youth Group Discussion Questions

Chapter One

1. Is Sam's reaction to starting a new school normal? Put yourself in her shoes, what would be the hardest thing to get used to, after having been through such a traumatic experience?
2. How are her new friends different from other friendships that she may have had in the past? How are they different from friends that you have in school?
3. How would you have reacted the about going to youth group if you were asked under the same circumstance?

Chapter Two

1. Why do you think that Uncle Joe is so quiet?
2. What is Sam's position on God, when Aunt Millie asks her about going to church?
3. During Sam's conversation with her aunt, what feelings rise up within her?
4. Why does Sam want to stay home instead of going to church?

Chapter Three

1. What are Sam and Jake's reaction to the youth room?

    a. What would your dream youth group or youth building look like?

2. How does Sam feel about the music that is playing?
3. How did you react the first time you came to youth group?
4. How is Jake handling all the change? What do we find out about how he is feeling at the end of the chapter?

Chapter Four

1. What triggers Sam's outburst?
2. Why is she so mean to Ms. Rose?
3. Why do you think Gloire wants to meet with Sam and Jake?
4. How should you handle a friend that has lost someone close to them?

    a. What are some ways to show them love?

Chapter Five

1. What is Sam's reaction to Gloire asking her about dancing?

    a. Why do you think she reacted that way? What are some of the things that you are passionate about?

2. How does Sam Sr. describe his wife? Why was Suzanne a special woman?
3. What made Ms. Yvonne's dance different from other dances that Sam had seen?
4. Why did Sam thank Samantha after the celebration service?

Chapter Six

1. Why is Sam going to the fridge on her own significant?
2. What makes Sam and Jake go up to the altar during Amped?
    a. What experience have you had with God?
3. How does dancing again make Sam feel?
4. What are some reasons that young people stay away from church?
    a. How can you reach out to your peers?

Chapter Seven

1. What surprise do Aunt Millie and Uncle Joe give to Jake and Sam?
2. What do we learn about Jade in this chapter?
3. Do you think Sam will be able to keep Jade's secret?
4. How do Mariah and Rachel handle the revelation?
    a. How would you handle a situation similar to Jade's? How would you react if one of your friends came to you with the same scenario?

Chapter Eight

1. What message did Jade get from Peter?
2. Why is Jade so upset after the incident in the bathroom?
3. How does Sam handle the situation in the bathroom?
    a. What is significant about her prayer?

Chapter Nine

1. What person comes back into Sam and Jake's life?
2. What is Sam's reaction to Grace's return?
    a. How do you think you would have reacted?
3. What was Aunt Millies' reaction to Sam's question about her staying with them?
4. How did Jade's father react to Jade's confession?
    a. How do you think your parents would react?
    b. How do you think God feels about Jade?

Chapter Ten

1. How did Sam and Jake respond to Grace coming over for dinner?
    a. Why do you think Jake's reactions are different than Sam's reaction to Grace's return?
2. What happened to Jade in this chapter?
3. How did Gloire react to Jade's confession?
    a. How was his reaction different from others? How was it similar to Sam's reaction?

Chapter Eleven

1. Why did Sam get upset about Matthew 18:21?
   a. Do you think you have the ability to carry out what God is telling us in this verse?
2. What do we learn about Uncle Joe?
   a. What are some qualities that Uncle Joe possesses?
3. What does Sam learn about forgiveness?
4. What was different about Sam's dancing now than when she used to dance for the School of The Arts?

Chapter Twelve

1. What happens at church in this chapter?
2. What does Sam feel in service that makes her go up front?
3. What do Sam and Jake learn about Grace in the diner?
   a. How do they respond?
4. What does Sam learn about the grace of God?
5. How can you apply this to your own life?